KEEP AND OTHER STORIES

Also by Peter Biles

Hillbilly Hymn

KEEP AND OTHER STORIES

Peter Biles

RESOURCE *Publications* · Eugene, Oregon

KEEP AND OTHER STORIES

Resource Publications
An Imprint of Wipf and Stock Publishers
199 W. 8th Ave., Suite 3
Eugene, OR 97401

www.wipfandstock.com

PAPERBACK ISBN: 978-1-6667-5326-4
HARDCOVER ISBN: 978-1-6667-5327-1
EBOOK ISBN: 978-1-6667-5328-8

09/19/22

For Dr. Anthony B. Bradley
Thank you for the encouragement.

"Love is something more stern and splendid than mere kindness."

—C.S. LEWIS

CONTENTS

Waking Up

Edgar emerged from the apartment at about 4 p.m., walking down the stone steps with the feeling that he'd just walked into an oven. The summer air hung heavy on the small birches along the street, and the sun shocked him and pried the sweat from his brow like medical prongs. He blinked, overwhelmed. The sidewalk, a blinding ribbon of white, must have just been poured again. The fire hydrant, not its usual rusty green, dazzled yellow. Edgar hesitated on the steps, rubbing his eyes, his face scrunched. He did not usually go outside at 4 p.m. in July. In the alleys between the apartments, air conditioner units dripped their cool excess of water on the shadowy pavement below—the perfect balm for the pigeons as they descended from their windowsills and gables. Construction workers sweated and hammered on a piece of bad road across the street. Flecks of bad road spattered the main part, where civics and CRVs and their phone absorbed drivers hurtled forth, unseeing, disregarding the vexed figure standing on the apartment steps in the unforgiving light of day.

Edgar thought about retreating into the apartment. Working online now, he could attune the atmosphere into a womb of comfort: the blanket draped over the chair, laptop positioned on the standing desk, although he rarely stood, the air conditioner pumping eternally behind him. The humidifier plumed every fifteen minutes. The kitchen sink held its usual repository. A pan with the egg still crusted on the bottom. Two plates lay stacked and smeared with peanut butter, another with marinara sauce. Spaghetti and PBJ sandwiches were the routine dinners. He brewed coffee in the mornings, and always made a cup too much for himself so the stuff made a black line of sediment in the pot, adding another stain on the glass, marking another day.

But he did not go back and did not give in. He blinked again, holding on to the rail as he felt the ground darken and adjust in front of him, and then stepped onto the sidewalk. Cars lined each side of the road, packed like sardines. Some were so precariously close that he wondered how on earth the driver was going to escape without scarring a bumper or two. The people were packed inside the houses too. There were not many families. There were many people like him on this street. They came out wearing sunglass and looking left and right with their golden doodles bounding against the leash, excited for its twenty minutes of measured freedom. They walked to shops or around the block, always with the head bent downward, a hand cradling the phone so the thumb could do its scrolling work, another on the leash—no attention applied to the avenue, the trees, the fire hydrant, the sweating workers, or Edgar.

Edgar walked until he reached the intersection, gleaning what shade he could from the leafy ornamental pear trees that lined the walk. He passed a young woman wearing sunglasses, pale tight jeans and a loose V-neck shirt, who ducked her head down when she passed him and then pulled out an iPhone too large for her pocket. Edgar paused to note the Catholic cathedral buttressing above the utilitarian cutout of a Target, and thought he saw pigeons circling its stony belfry, searching for a route to the bell.

The cross traffic went unimpeded at the intersection, and he felt even more oppressed by the heat and the brightness as he returned his gaze in front of him and decided to cross the street to get to the other block, where better shade and solitude awaited. So far, or so he felt, his attempt to be confronted radically by the real world wasn't working. Not that he didn't *want* it to work. He felt he lacked the ability to really see anything in front of him, drowned as he was in the thought, *It is so freaking hot out here.* The impulse to look at his phone was irresistible, but he had left it his den, along with the Air pods, Apple watch, and organic soy chips.

He put one foot forward into the road, stepped back quickly as an Altima jounced by, reverberating with Shakira. He tried again. A Ford truck was approaching conservatively to his left, so he made a break for it without considering his right.

Do you know what it is like to be hit by a car going thirty-seven miles an hour in a twenty-five zone? It is not enough to kill you but plenty enough to thrown you in the air like a saucer of pizza dough, a gymnast attempting a backflip but becoming a corpse in midair. That's what Edgar felt like as he swooned at the apex of his propulsion—a conscious mind in a body that might as well have been a hunk of dough. He fell on his side on the opposite sidewalk, so if anything, he had succeeded in crossing the street. His body below his waist felt like it didn't exist, as if he'd been shot up into space and shed the lower capsule, only to plunge back to earth as a disgrace to the mission for Mars.

The car that had hit him, a Subaru Cross-trek, slowed down to thirty-one miles per hour and stopped at the following intersection, detained by an interminable red light. The three minutes it sat there, the whole vehicle stewed in conflict and contemplation. The driver's head was still, hands clenched and trembling on the wheel. She had killed the music and dropped her phone with her friend still on the line chattering about a Netflix binge and a breakup for which she wasn't responsible for. Edgar, meanwhile, rolled on his back and looked at the tree branches above him as the pain from his broken legs started to catch up to his adrenaline. He could feel the pain now. Now it really did feel like a car had hit him, like the sidewalk, white as a winter moon, the yellow fire hydrant reminding him of the taste of mustard, the sweating and hammering men getting down into the grit of the sidewalk, the pigeons bathing in air conditioner, all fomented and intensified on his forehead and eyes and on his whole body in overwhelming weight.

The Subaru drove away slowly after brutal hesitation under the green light by the closed doors of the cathedral. She must've glanced at the pillared inscription of the church and felt some kind of piety, for she dialed the number, absolved herself of the guilt, and sped off as if the green light were God's way of saying she'd done her duty. It was strange that the world kept going by outside her window as casually and comfortably as it did.

The ambulance swerved the streets. The traffic divided and veered off the road in condolence and respect. A couple of the construction workers knelt next to Edgar, looking concerned through their sweating faces, trying to get through to him, telling him help was coming, and they were there for him. Edgar was not thinking about his phone or the terrible heat when they cradled him through the back doors of the ambulance.

He thought he'd never seen a human face so clearly as the one telling him to stay with it—the nurse's hand kept him connected to the single block of world he had walked through, been pummeled by, that he would return to.

BROKEN ARM

SINCE birth I've been able to conveniently remove my left arm and have it turn into a violin. Now I am not a musical person. Anyone can tell you that, not least of all my dog Mildred, my comatose chihuahua. I've always thought it stupid of me to buy a violin when I can go ahead and pluck one right off my body. But I've also always considered it a real cruel joke of nature to be given this appendage when every fool knows you need two hands to play a violin! So I used to sulk about it wonder why the heck this happened to me, why God, apparently being musical himself, would consign me to a violin that I could hold in one hand. Who knew?

No one knew of my condition, not even my parents, to my understanding. I was in and out of orphanages until the age of ten and had the sort of disposition that naturally excused me from society or friendship, so hardly anyone got around to even knowing my *name* until I moved to this frigid, desolate metropolis where the money is worth nothing and the men worth even less. The city was not always a rabble of vapid politicians and crumbling families and fool's errands like myself, all wandering around its bankrupt avenues decrepit and morally gutted. Apparently, it was once a bright, festive place. The history books, if you can find them, will tell you the same. But I don't know. History matters little if the people have no will to remember it. And when you don't remember, you can't think. That's all the wisdom I have for you. The rest is just a stupid story about my stupid pointless violin arm that had no use or function whatsoever.

A girl begged on my streets in those days. Times were bad. Politically, every man was a straw man, and every woman a straw woman. One movement of wind, and they fell. You know how that goes. Economically, well, I won't get into boring inflation details. Point is a girl begged on my streets in those days. She was about fifteen years old, always wearing the same dirty dress and going around barefoot and hatless. She might've been a pretty girl once, or still was, behind the smudges of coal soot on her face and her ratty mess of hair. She slept on my doorstep most nights, wrapped in her shawl. My apartment was smaller than a goat stall, so you understand I had no room to put her up in. Yes, that's right–I plead guilty along with the innkeeper who turned away the Mother of our Lord, but what was I (or he) supposed to do?

It bothered my conscience that the girl slept out there every night. I couldn't imagine how'd she would survive another bitter winter out on the streets. In those days, people turned up frozen in the alleyways, their last expressions immortalized, their last postures made into statues. The photographs I saw of suffering people made it hard to feel at ease with one's own relative comfort. But I didn't know what I could do for her.

One day as I was coming home from the shop I clerked at, she sat hunched and morose on the steps hugging her knees and staring gloomily at the ground. She was dirty and unruly as usual, and I muttered a brief "hullo" while fumbling for the keys.

"What a rotten day," I heard her say.

I stopped next to her and replied, "May I ask why?"

"They closed the last music store in the city," she said, not looking up at me. "It was the best store around. It was my favorite thing to do to look at the instruments in the window and hear the people play them inside. They would let me play the instruments too, sometimes."

"What instrument do you play?" I asked.

"The violin," she sighed. "I love the violin. The cello too, but mainly the violin. You don't really hear much music anymore. All you hear are cars honking, people shouting, all the movies and lights and noise. No music."

As you can imagine I had developed quite the troubled scowl on my face. A violin!

"The violin, eh?" I said, turning back to my set of keys.

"That's right." Now she craned her neck to look at me. "You don't happen to have one yourself, do you?"

I breathed in, suddenly conscious of how cold it was, noticing the frost on her eyelashes, the blueness beginning to crowd in on her lips. I sighed.

"You're cold," I muttered, helping her to her feet. "You're not usually here at this hour, are you?"

"No, not usually." Her teeth chattered, and I didn't know where she could even sit inside the apartment. My dog, Mildred, was a comatose chihuahua who spent her days snoozing in a shoebox at the foot of my cot. She had no sense of reality whatsoever, and so probably wouldn't mind sharing her meager quarters. I unlocked the door, the girl at my elbow, and regretted to discover it was hardly any warmer inside.

"There's talk of having to cut off the power to the city," the girl notified me.

"Oh, excellent!" I went down on my knees and blew into the open grate of my woodstove, resurrecting a dying ember and setting more kindling on until we had a healthy flame dancing through the venting.

"It isn't much," I apologized. "You see that although I wish you weren't so cold out there at night, I couldn't give you a place to stay. Not unless you want to sleep standing up."

"It isn't much," she said, nodding in agreement. "But thank you for letting me in." I remembered the folding chair that I kept hidden in the closet, which was about the size of a gutter bucket, and unfolded it next to her.

"Cheers. Do you like coffee?"

The girl hesitated as if she wasn't sure. She decided that yes, she did. She had enjoyed it once when they were giving out hot chocolate and coffee at the music store. She drank in the hot bitterness, felt its warmth spread in her belly and to her arms, even to the tips of her fingers.

I started the coffee on my single burner stove, thinking about my violin arm, then trying not to think about it, then thinking, *She plays the violin! Dear heavens, the violin!*

She took the cup of coffee once it was finished and sat on the edge of the bed next to the motionless chihuahua. She didn't drink from it, but held the cup tightly with both hands, close to her chest. I supposed then that I should offer some vittles.

"I've just a pea's worth of chicken soup leftover, if you want some of that," I said.

She was quiet a moment, as if realizing she hadn't trespassed someone's hospitality to this extent in a long time, or ever in her life for that matter. And she nodded, choosing to be honest. "Yes please."

I put the soup on and added the last of the timber to the woodstove. It would die out before nightfall.

"Where is it you work?" the girl asked me as I leaned against the foot-long counter.

"I work at a meat store. Butcher work." I rubbed my hands together, feeling their callousness, their use.

"That's a job for two hands, isn't it," she said in a low whisper that sounded as if she had come to some terrible realization.

"Indeed it is." Who could expect a butcher to cut a slab of sirloin in half with just one hand? Possible, surely, but far from ideal.

The girl ate the soup silently, but was done with it in seconds, and handed me back the bowl.

"Well," she said, sliding herself off the bed. "I guess I'd better get going."

"Already? Well. If you say so, I suppose."

I reached for the door with my left hand, and granted, this is a door known to jam and stick when I try to open it, but I was going for courtesy, for hospitality, seeking to make up for the many months I'd withheld it. And the door stuck, as usual, lurching and grunting, and so I pulled smartly on the handle with gritted teeth, realizing a moment too late what this would do. The arm popped out of its socket and turned into the dark wooded violin, bow tucked under the strings. The instrument fell unimpeded, giving a wounded hum as it met the floor. The girl jumped back from the scene with a scream and I scrambled to pick up the violin, rejoining it to my body so it turned back into flesh.

"Very well then, guess I'll be seeing you around!" I laughed, ashen faced.

The girl, brows furrowed, pointed at my arm and said, "What . . . b-but . . . I saw it, the violin, it came out of you. Out of your arm!"

"Nonsense," I cooed, trying to flank her out the door. "You must be seeing things." I noticed a suspicious gleam in the girl's ruddy face, and before I could even call to Mildred for assistance, she had snatched the arm and fled into the street with the violin and bow in hand.

"You there!" I cried, one armed in the doorway. "Thief! Thief! Bring that back!" I ran into the street after her, but she had already vanished into some secluded alleyway, no doubt jigging for joy over her contemptuous luck.

"Police!" I cried. But the police were a weak presence in that part of the city, and most likely wouldn't believe that a dirty beggar girl had stolen my arm right off my body. Certainly I wouldn't believe such an absurd story if someone told it to *me*.

The best I could do then was snoop around the alleyways for a spell and tramp back home through the cold, hoping no one would notice my missing arm. The folks at work would all be asking how I lost it, so I'd have to devise some kind of clever tale. Goodness, now *everyone* would look at me funny. Or shield their children's ogling eyes, prevent them from making brash comments about the lack.

"That brat!" I fumed once I was back inside. "You see! That's what I get for being so called 'hospitable.' Try to love your neighbor as yourself and you find yourself missing an arm. What's the good in that, I ask!" I threw the rest of the coffee away and hurled the pot of soup against the wall so even the comatose chihuahua twitched an ear. I huddled near the woodstove even as it started to fade, needing more wood, needing more of everything all the time—and now, needing an arm.

There was a thicket on the edge of town that folks often visited to gather kindling. Sometimes you could see a line of people filing through the snow towards the trees, blowing into their fists and looking bitterly up at the sky. I stood up, put on my trench coat, and observed myself in my six-inch-wide mirror above the sink. The left arm looked empty enough. And it was getting dark outside.

So I shuffled out into the snow and made my bitter way down Wiley Street, turning the corner with a few other wretches, and soon found myself on the narrow path towards the thicket. Behind us, the city was a flickering lightbulb, sashed in snow, a ghost town. You could hear arguments coming from within its streets, cars hitting each other, people hitting each other. Removed from the city, my feet trudging through the snow, and the coming quiet weighing heavy before me, I wondered sullenly about the meaning of my existence. Does this sound bleak and obvious? The others around me must have been wondering too, to be walking along a thin path of ice, hedged in by frozen sage and wheat grass, when there was a time we were all around our fireplaces together–yes, even the beggars among us invited in to warm their hands and arms. Now no one spoke. We rubbed our hands together, or those of us with only one hand to spare rubbed it up and down the thigh. The sunset shown purple and meager beyond the thicket. A deer pranced through the field, looking like a skeletal shadow in the dimness. People were coming out of the thicket holding bundles of kindling in their arms.

As soon as I entered the fold of trees the air grew darker to the point of stumbling. Without the use of both my arms, I lost balance and went headlong in the snow. Some fellow gatherers snickered nearby. Grasping a limber ash tree for support, I rose to my feet again. Missing a part of one's body doesn't come without resistance. I found myself thrashing around, my mind still convinced I was a man with two arms instead of just one.

"The man's a fool–forgot to bring a lantern," said an old man standing nearby. The lantern he carried issued a yellow glow on the snow, showing the broken sticks he was picking up. Although he called me a fool, he sounded like he was chuckling, kindly even. I propped myself on my single elbow, heaving for breath, watching the old man move slowly with the lantern. He wore a cloak, sort of archaic with the hood over his head, and there was a basket on his back.

He turned around, holding the lantern above his face so the creases of his features looked timelessly engraved. His eyebrows made shadows over his eyes but a hooked nose appeared out of the darkness.

"You're struggling in the snow there," he remarked, slowly, thoughtfully, putting a hand to his mouth.

"You really think so?" I muttered, standing up and brushing myself clean.

"Something isn't right," the old man said, squinting at me. It was just my luck to encounter some sort of diabolical wizard on this day of unfortunate events. You will have noticed that I can be a pessimistic, self-pitying type, and can turn even good events into curses if I have will enough.

"You need help," he said, as if finally deciding.

I glared at him in the darkness, suddenly finding him very unwelcome company. "No," I said.

"You were thrashing in the snow like a wounded beast," said the old man. I could tell he was peering at my left arm's lifeless sleeve.

"I don't need your help. Thanks." But I wasn't thankful.

"Very well. But you ought not come alone in your state. Not at this hour."

"I don't need anyone telling me what I can and can't do." I paused, my hand growing numb in the snow. "I've just had a terrible day."

"Sorry to hear it."

"I hate that I don't have an arm." The sentence just slipped as if had been waiting there all day. Perhaps my whole life, in a way, you know.

"You hate it because you don't know what to do with yourself without it?"

"You don't know me. You don't know what I've been through. Where I've been, who has hurt me." After hesitating with a hand on my hip, I chose to spit out the ridiculous truth. "Just today my arm was stolen from me. That's right. Plucked right off! The brat ran away with it for her own purposes."

He didn't seem like he either believed or disbelieved me. He just listened, and replied, "Perhaps those purposes were noble, but the means ignoble. But I'm sorry."

I started wondering why I was wasting my time bantering and stooped to pick up some kindling. This is harder than you might expect when you have just one arm. In fact, it's impossible to get a grip on anything larger than the width of your palm if you're trying to keep a woodstove going all night. Growling under my breath, I tried balancing a broken branch in the crook of my elbow and against my shoulder.

"Do you need help?" the old man asked.

"No!" I snarled, retreating a few steps into the dimness. "I don't need any damned help."

"You're bitter like the winter wind," he said, straightening up with the lantern dangling from a couple fingers by his knees. "You need a hand. Literally, it turns out. And you've forgotten a lantern. Do you want to return cold to your apartment, and risk being mugged by ruffians on the trail?"

I gathered what kindling I had managed and started strutting out of the forest away from the light. The wind gnashed outside the trees, although the spread of stars had rubied itself across the sky and beckoned my eyes beyond my selfish little purview. The trail was empty and quiet, and the city gave distant cries not quite unlike the lonely howling of a wolf. The universe seemed like it was spinning in correspondence to my fragile state of mind, wobbling at the edge of a cliff, threatening to tumble over into poverty, nothingness. The first step on the icy path, the grass rustled and shifted. The old man had prophesied correctly. Not a minute later and I was sprawled on the ground without my coat and kindling, blood streaming from a wound in my temple and a general sense of bamboozlement settling over my whole existence. The thieves, and I don't know how many there were, robbed and beat me, mocking my armless body and scuttling away into the darkness like spiders.

"A fool," I muttered. "Just an armless, bitter fool, like the man said." This was the predicament: a bad day had gone worse, and it was my fault no two ways about it. I laid there in the grass, stewing in aches and breathing shallowly, with the same spread of stars above me provoking my awe even as my head pulsed. It mocked me with its majesty. That's all shame is, I suppose—the response we mistakenly practice when beauty mocks all our finite, weak semblances simply by being what it is. Swallow the shame and you swallow yourself with it, until all that's left are those stars, but strangely enough you still feel grounded to snow and wheat grass, not annihilated, not nothing. Maybe you're even smiling once the medicine goes down.

A few minutes later the old man tramped down the path. The glow of the lantern shed itself on my bleeding form and he stooped next to me, lantern clutched in his teeth, and gathered me into his arms to carry me home as if he'd expected to find me there. I don't know how he knew where I lived, but the next morning I woke up next to a crackling woodstove and a note lying on top of Mildred the comatose chihuahua. It simply read: *Helped people help people. Savvy?*

I got up, feeling strangely rested, more than I ever had in my life. The fire was still healthy and crackling, with a stack of extra kindling setting besides the stove. Goodness, there was an even a readymade omelet laying warm on the griddle! The old man had gone to some radical lengths. I warmed myself even further next to the stove and ate the omelet with my bare hand. I picked up the coffee and put it to my lips, about to enjoy its comforts, when something scratched my door, as if a box was being set down for delivery. I opened the door and found the violin, then realizing with a hard shock what this meant, looked eagerly up and down the street. There was no sign of the beggar girl. She had played music in the streets all right, and brought back a bundle of dough to prove it. I went back inside, scratching my head and quite honestly reliving the old sweet shame I'd sat in the night before. Steal? From me?

I searched for her all day. She wasn't on the doorstep that night, and the next morning I even asked the neighbors if they had seen her.

"What are you interested in a poor beggar girl for?" my neighbor Mr. Chops asked me irritably as he searched for his keys.

"She gave me something and I'm trying to return the favor," I said.

"A favor, eh? Heh! What kind of favor was it, might I ask? He-hehe–trying to get her to give it to ye again, is that it?" No one else on the block said they had seen her.

With two arms again I found myself oddly wishing to give one away. I made trips to the thicket for kindling, always looking out for the old man and never finding him. I wondered if I had imagined the encounter. Months passed and turned into another winter, and I was sitting next to the stove and smoking my pipe with the comatose chihuahua spread in perfect peace on my lap. It was December thirteenth. My miniscule Christmas tree was propped up in the corner, a sloppy angel figurine atop it, with even the sound of some carolers echoing down the street. Things were getting a little better. Politically I mean. Not every man a straw man, not every woman a straw woman, vulnerable to the wind. Someone knocked on the door just as I was dozing off to sleep, and the thought of the beggar girl came to mind. Maybe she was wearing a beautiful petticoat. Maybe she had married rich and lived in an enormous mansion on the edge of town. Maybe she was the Queen of England, somehow. Flinging open the door, however, I was met with an unexpected sight: a little boy no older than five holding out of his hands with his head bowed. He was holding a smashed violin in one hand. I didn't even see the bow.

"Well?" I asked.

"Excuse me, sir," he said. "They've broken my music maker. The bullies. They broke it. For no reason at all. Won't you fix it? A certain old chap and beggar girl told me you're good with violins."

He offered me the mess, surprised to see me smile and pop off my arm.

"I'll do you one better, son," I said, and told him to cherish the instrument forever.

HAMAT AND THE BLUE WHALE

I LIKE to think now that the great flood saved me. I would have died that night. Instead, everyone else died that night.

I was walking home on the secret path because there was a bloody brawl on the main road in the town behind me. The brawl started when a man became jealous of another man with the woman and the woman failed to devote herself with either man, and the men happened to be of the kind of stature to attract opponents and proponents, and most of them if not all of them will be dead by the morning. They were all also very drunk.

The silence fell heavily on the secret path. The air had grown cold and staunch, and I could see my breath illuminated by the moonlight coming down through the trees. The branches were brittle and dead, with the remaining leaves trembling like limp flags of a lost nation in the wind. I wrapped my tunic more tightly around myself, thinking about the day, about the brawl, about my own pathetic life. Don't mistake me—I almost joined in. There was a knife waiting in my boot and the same violence and love for death brewing in my head, just like the rest of those fools. But the moment the first fist was thrown and the first corpse got flung as high as the temple and landed like an omen in the ditch, I thought to myself, "That corpse might as well be me, and pretty soon that will be all of us" and so I left. The cries of despair sang like a discordant choir in the night behind me. These brawls hit the town just about every night. Men and women would be crawling home in pieces after their conclusion. So many family feuds. So many daggers in the back, gnashing teeth and wicked gleams in the eyes. Hatred marked the air as apparently as the temple's burnt human sacrifices. It was the town. It was, so far as anyone could tell, the whole world.

I reached the top of the hill and looked back over the town as the clouds gathered in mass behind me to the north, and the wind got a sharp edge to it that spoke of disaster and an end to everything it touched. The lights in the town intensified. Buildings burned like torched hands begging to be put out. Only parts of the town could ever be rebuilt before the next riot set yet another district on fire, so I suppose that soon the town will be reduced to ash. The smoke glazed a portion of the universe foregrounded by the village. The stars were too monumental to be intimidated by the smoke, sporting their helixes and milky wreaths like forests unstained by earthly pollutants.

I started down the hill towards the cottage. The lantern lit up the porch, just as it was left. I was not expecting destruction yet, and not in the manner it would come. I still needed time. I needed time to decide about Laurel, for one. She still had it in her head that women were given in marriage, and that not all men, because of some conviction of conscience, visited the prostitution houses that were more prevalent than homes in our village.

"Hamat, we must be married," she told me. "We must be married and leave this terrible place before we are killed. Don't you see, Hamat? Something tells me that we will be killed if we stay." Laurel. She kept herself high up and out of sight during the brawls. When I visited her, she only wanted to talk about leaving.

"We cannot leave," I told her. "The gods have given me many omens of gambling prizes if I will only stay and worship them in the temples for a bit longer. Then I will be rich, and will have power over all these drunken fools, and I will buy you everything. Don't you see, my apple?"

"I do not want everything, Hamat! Only you! And only to leave this place!" She knew very little about the real world.

And of course there were my debts to settle. I had amassed many in the past few months, but I also had visions of the gods beckoning me to stay, promising wealth and happiness and fortune if I would only keep flipping the coin and muttering their mantras. I must pray to Shepikah for guidance of the coin—and believe that every time this fails it is because Shepikah's devilish cousin Srad, who is a devil and has only a temple meant for weak people too cowardly to risk and gamble, is tampering with the result. With Laurel I intended to use her for as long as the need demanded, or the desire for her beauty subsided, and with the debts—Srad would not entangle me any longer. Men can harness the gods as long as they chant long and hard enough. It is a science, they say.

But I had no time to do any of these things. Before I reached the cottage, the wind howled, pellets of rain abused the trail before me, and I found myself entangled in a tree branch ten feet off the ground as the deluge broke out. The sky might as well have opened its vaults by the command of some angry god. The moon hid itself, the world went black, including the lights from the towns, and in only moments water swirled at my feet.

I scrambled up higher to the top of the tree, prayed for the gods to relent, and did my best to shield the wall of rain and wind from my eyes. The water rose, erasing the cottage and the hill, uprooting trees and livestock, dividing houses and churning temples upside down so driftwood and human beings went undistinguished in the melee. A piece of fencing hit me in the head and I fell into the depths, while somewhere beyond the clouds the universe beamed on. And the gods were not looking at the earth.

But, then, light. Water. Air.

I woke up on the back of a great blue whale. It skimmed close enough to the surface of the water for me to breathe freely. The providence of the gods adorned me, so it seemed. The rain continued but gently, and as far as the eye could see in there spread a gray expanse of water, with no sign of land.

The blue whale must have noticed that I had propped myself on an elbow. It slowed to a stop, arching itself backward so I had to hold on to one of his crustacean moles, and said, "You're awake then," in a voice so deep it hurt my ears and shook my heart.

I blinked. "Yes," I replied. "You're a talking whale, then?"

"Only a whale. You're fortunate to be alive." And then it leveled out again. Thirty minutes later it resurfaced. "Name?"

"Hamat."

"Hamat." Then back under.

I blinked in wonder again and kept on wondering. I wondered how far the flood reached. I wondered if my whole nation was underwater or if I had simply floated into the ocean. I wondered where my clothes were but at the same time didn't mind being naked in the open with the rain beating and kneading my skin. There was no longer anyone to see my nakedness. An hour more passed, and the remains of an enormous ship appeared. Driftwood, masts, chests with unknown contents went bobbing among the flotsam, and corpses floated face down in the water. The whale raised its head and said, "You are not the only survivor."

"Where are the others?" I shouted. "Can you take me to them?" But the whale did not answer.

One of the chests floated nearby, unlocked and askew just enough for me to catch a glint of ruby and gold inside. My eye gleamed. That much wealth would seat me miles above any town brawl. "Stop!" I cried, batting the whale's head. "We must stop."

"Why? For the gold?"

"It's more than I've ever seen in my life! It would be a disaster leaving it to sink into the sea!"

"Everything sinks. Everything dies. Or almost everything. That was the deal."

"I'm not dead! Not yet!" Still the whale swam on so I had to decide between the gold and my own skin. I watched the treasure chest float weakly on for a spell until it dipped under the waves and was lost forever.

Evening set in and the rain thinned. The clouds above parted, revealing crowns and myriads of planets and stars, though the surrounding horizons were still beating with storms. The gods must still be quarrelling and abusing each other with arrows of lightning and slingshots of rain.

"It's quiet and clear here. The only place of quiet on the whole earth." The whale heaved a heavy sigh and added, "I brought you here so you can speak. Speak to me what was good about your human life."

I paused, sudden anger welling up inside of me. "You tell me not to ask questions when I am atop a blue whale on a world turned to water—and now you want answers from me! I will pray to Hawaptu, god of the sea, so long as I think he will save me."

"Hawaptu did not save you," murmured the whale. "Now be calm. See the ocean? It has calmed."

"Well, what do you want from me? I could have died in the flood. Now I will die on top of a whale. Die then. Die now. It makes no difference."

"What if you had lived?" asked the whale. I saw one of its inky black eyes, heavily lidded by time and mollusks, intently settled on the horizon.

"Do you mean what if it had never flooded?"

The whale said nothing. A parade of dolphins leaped in harmony some cubits away and left quiet ripples in their wake.

I sighed. "Ah. I don't know what I would have done. Died there, most likely, died with a cursed knife in my throat. Do you know that my kind are violent, whale? That we brawl and beat and kill? That no man, woman or child is safe no matter where they walk?"

"It does not matter," said the whale. "They are all gone."

"All? What of the survivors?"

Again, I was given no answer. And it then occurred to me that everyone I had ever known was probably dead—no tree or tower or temple was tall enough to escape the flood. My parents, old and wizened, were dead. My sister, Malat, dead. Laurel was dead. Her loss, one death among millions, was like a single mark of ink in a web of letters, and the mark became white and rose off the page before me. "We should be married, Hamat," her voice chimed. "We should be married and leave this horrible place, or be killed." The words made me feel very alone.

"You are suddenly quiet," said the whale.

"You don't answer my questions. I don't answer yours. It is simple," I said.

"Well then. Shall I take a deep dive into the depths and leave you to yourself then?"

"Better that than dying slowly in your presence," I grumbled. Suddenly, the whale turned its nose and plunged downward, making me tumble headfirst into the frigid water. The water clashed back together in the place where its enormous body went down, dragging me underneath in a vortex. I do not know how to swim. I thrashed my arms and legs, spouting curses against the whale and stars and the gods, feeling my weight pull me slowly under until there was only blackness and a feeling of terrible loneliness. Darkness and loneliness. Maybe I was the last human to choke. The last one to curse the divine going under, cursing until the bitter end. But amidst the thoughts, a deeper impulse banged at my heart. *Help me! I'm dying. Help me, help me!* I shouted the words underwater, grasping for the ocean surface, grasping for the life I knew I didn't want to leave, the life that was not worth having. I must have sunk thirty feet down, thrashing and wailing, until I felt my back come up against something hard and steady. The whale's nose held me in place, and we ascended until bursting through the surface. The whale spouted and ducked beneath me, coming back up with my naked body straddled over its back. I gasped for breath and wept aloud.

"You were saying?" said the whale.

"Gods," I moaned, half in relief, half in terror.

"Your gods are not listening to you," said the whale, turning on its back and placing me on its stomach with its enormous fins. "Feel the warmth of my underside, human. And speak to me." I shivered in a ball on the soft belly, soon warming up and losing the former terror of being trapped underwater.

"What is there to speak?" I began, sitting up and wiping my hair from my eyes. "There was nothing to live for, nothing to die for. There were words and then there was blood. There were never words leading to laughter. Only circus laughter when a weak fool was being chased in the ring by some beast. Laughter at death. We have a love for death."

Silence.

"But if I must speak, now that I must die in the middle of the sea upon a whale, then so be it. What if I had lived, you ask? I would have married Laurel, if you must know. No one knew of my weakness for her—how I was fond of her presence in a way that the brothel houses could never match. I do not know what to call it."

"In whale language, we call it love," said the whale softly.

"Love, eh? It isn't a word in our vocabulary. Anyway. If you must interrogate me, I would say to Laurel, 'Yes, let us marry and leave this terrible place, where we will most certainly die in the violence. Yes, let us love one another if we can.' If love is what you'd call it."

"Would you do anything else?"

"I don't know! What else is there to say?" I paused, head in my hands, sorrow welling in my heart.

"Perhaps that I would promise to stop putting myself in the debt of other men, and listening to the gods. The gods, it is widely known, are just as evil as men but can be bought by promises and prayers. But here I am. Drowning. It no longer matters."

The whale said nothing, but I knew it listened.

"I left the brawl because I didn't want to die. But why live? I do not know. Even if the rains hadn't killed, we would have killed each other. Maybe it is more pitiable to live than to die when death is the only intent of the heart. God! A flood may have been a mercy to those bloodstained fools. But why my salvation? Why did you save me?"

"I saw your floating body in the depths, alone and dying," said the whale. "I thought you may have been dead already. But I thought to myself—why not save the human, an air breather like myself, and see if he really is as wicked as the aqua maids tell me. Tell me, have you killed? Have you plundered? Have you raped?"

"Why deny it?" I cried. "Everyone pillaged. They pillaged human bodies and the body of the earth. I told you—destruction was always in our eyes, and bloodshed on our minds. You should not have saved me. You should have let me die with everyone else. I deserve nothing more."

"Sleep, Hamat," the whale said. "Speak later. Perhaps your fast is over. Sleep on the warmth of my back. There is nothing to be done about it now."

I slept and dreamed of the green eyes of Laurel and green pastures where many streams flowed and met—like the waters of a paradise long lost. When I woke up, I laid on the back of the whale and a brass sun was shining overhead. Beside me, just above the water, a spritely green leaf of a tree pulsed with life. I picked if off and smelled its leaves, which budded with white flowers gilded with gold along its fragrant rims. "The water subsides," I marveled.

"Did you think it would rain forever?" the whale said. "And look now! A dove is descending." And truly, a white dove settled on the back of the whale's head and studied me with a cocked head. "The green?" I said, brows furrowed. The dove snatched the bough with its beak and flew away like a holy sprite. And even then, leagues away towards where the bird soared, I saw the figure of a great ship sailing.

THE BLACK SQUIRREL

OLD Mr. Travis sat on his porch smoking a cigar reading the Chicago Tribune, though his lazy eye beheld the child, Lil Ronny, zooming down the sidewalk with the force of a young wildebeest. He remembered. He had meant to shovel up the black squirrel and throw it away in the Waste Corporation bin in his driveway but the morning paper distracted him. The child hurtled down the sidewalk on his scooter and paid no mind to the loose concrete and pieces of mulch in his path. He wore his lime green shorts, wore no shirt, and trained his eyes indubitably on the path before him, like a great battle beckoned him towards impossible foes. Mr. Travis had left that morning to buy a cup of coffee, and when he came back, found the squirrel dead by his fledgling oak tree that stood between the sidewalk and the road. It didn't seem to have been run over. It was just lying there, a paw covering its eye and its tail curled around its body as a makeshift shroud of Tehran. Mr. Travis thought it might be asleep, but he prodded it with its cane so it rigidly laid on its back, and he knew.

Stuffing the paper into the cupholder of his lawn chair, fearing that the boy would trip on the squirrel, he achingly rose to his feet, picked up his cane, and searched for the shovel among the hoes and uprooted posts by his small garden of tomato, cucumber, and squash. Still Lil Ronny careened. This would be a close race. Ronny's mother once told Mr. Travis that her boy wasn't as lionhearted as he made out to be. Said he had been devastated by the death of a moth in the garage, gave it a funeral and mourned like a tribal leader over its slaughtered young. So maybe more was at stake than just a nasty fall. Mr. Travis got the old shovel and scuttled as fast as he could to the tree, mapping out his trajectory: squirrel to trashcan, then shovel to soil, like he was simply tending the property. "I'll just get that taken care of, then I'll work on that weed-eater in the garage," he muttered to himself. He never got around to working on the weed-eater.

Just out of the gate, Mr. Travis, having underestimated the speed and cunning of this scooter borne child, was bowled over by the seven-year-old like an antelope at the mercy of a tiger, and was laid out on his back with the branches of the oak shivering in the wind above him. He and the squirrel lay side by side. It was like he was back in his army days, shell shocked with a domesticated natural world still pretending to protect him. *Lordy*, he thought, *I'm old.* Where Lil Ronny ended up, he didn't know, but through the ringing in his ears, he heard: "Ah my hand!! Oh! Ah! Mr. Travis! You didn't die, did you? Are you died?"

"No, I'm not died," he said, trying to chuckle and sitting up holding the back of his head. Ronny's red scooter lay upside down against the oak tree, its back wheel still spinning. Lil Ronny, however, was more worried he may have just committed manslaughter, and was already busy helping the old man to his feet, repeating, "I'm sorry Mr. Travis, I'm sorry!"

"You're okay, son, you're okay."

"I help you get in the house, I help you!"

"Well, I'm sure I'll be fine."

"No, no, no, I help you!"

The child was insatiable. It had been a long time since Mr. Travis had met someone who simply wouldn't take *no* for an answer. Lil Ronny held the old man's hand and led him up the front steps, all the while with Mr. Travis thinking about the scooter and the squirrel. *He's going to see it no matter what I do now*, he thought to himself. *I should have shoveled it up this morning after coffee.*

"So, no school today, eh?" Mr. Travis asked once they were on the porch.

"Nah. Teachers are mad at the governor or something."

"Ah. Sounds about right." He noticed then that the knuckle on one the boy's index finger was strawberry red with blood, and that he had a palliative scrape between his flabby pectorals.

"Say, you took quite a fall yourself," he added, opening the screen door. "C'mon in . . . I got Band-Aids. And juice."

The boy was hesitant at the door, casting a glance back at his scooter, but went inside and idled quietly in the foyer where he was met with the smell of books, leather, pipe smoke, after shave tonic, and a general musk that some old people's houses accumulate with age. Mr. Travis noticed his curiosity and let him hold the jackknife he was ogling on the piano mantle.

"Wow," he whispered. "I've never held a knife before. Mom won't let me! Do you got swords? Do you got rifles and swords?"

"Well, no, not quite, son," the old man laughed. "Here, let's get you fixed up in the bathroom and then I'll pour you some juice."

"Juice? What about whiskey?"

"You watch a lot of western movies, don't you, kiddo?"

"Yeah. Used to with Dad, anyway."

Mr. Travis led him to the bathroom and took out his little plastic First Aid Kit, sorting through the compartments and taking out a Band-Aid for the knuckle, hoping he would have to use the restroom to give him time to dispose of the squirrel. Should have offered the juice to begin with.

"Thanks," said Ronny after the bandage was on and his "chest wound," as he preferred to call it, had been patched up.

"Need to use the restroom?"

"No. Do you? Mom said old people have to use the restroom a lot."

"No, I don't have to." Although he did. Ronny returned quickly to the living room. Meanwhile, Mr. Travis shut the bathroom door and sat down, with relief, upon the toilet with his drawers dropped. He wondered about the last time someone had stepped foot into his house. It wasn't decent enough for a dinner party, but apparently this child considered it a jungle gym of intrigue. He bowed his head, interlocking his fingers and studying the lines of the linoleum floor. Antoinette, if she were here, would give the boy a sandwich and lemonade. If it were winter, she would have provided him with a spread of hot chocolate and cookies, and set him next to the fire, where she would encourage Mr. Travis to tell stories about his time in Europe. *He wouldn't want to hear that stuff, would he?*

Mr. Travis finished and stood. He heard nothing. Was the boy reading a tome from the bookshelf? In the living room, he expected Ronny to be investigating the various blades on the jackknife, but instead found that he was holding a small black and white portrait, which usually sat enthroned at the center of the mantle above the fireplace. Mr. Travis stopped short and said, "What are you doing?"

The boy was quick to realize he'd picked up a forbidden object. "Oh, sorry Mr. Travis. Here I'll put it back."

"No! You might drop it." Mr. Travis took the portrait and set it back in its place.

"Sorry."

Mr. Travis grunted. *Kids.*

"Who's the lady in the picture, Mr. Travis?" Ronny still had his eyes fixed on the portrait, almost as if he was convinced he was looking at a real woman. She wore her wedding dress, eyes lowered on her bouquet of lilies, her black shoulders exposed though half hidden by her veil. Mr. Travis swallowed and cracked his fingers. Ronny just stared. Why would he lie to a child? Does it help them?

"She was my wife, son. Long time ago."

"What happened to her? Why isn't she here?"

Ronny's mother probably didn't approve of his scooter. In fact, Mr. Travis was fairly sure she had confiscated it only for Ronny to double his efforts to find it again. There were cars in the street that might swerve, not to mention strangers and rogue dogs and dead squirrels lying next to the sidewalk. Anything could go wrong for a kid on a scooter. An old man might walk out of his yard any second, causing a collision. God forbid the child would scrape a knuckle and feel pain. And God *further* forbid the old man take him in and give him a discourse on cancer and death.

Mr. Travis sighed. If his mother called about the wounds, he would take the blame. "She got sick when we were still young and died not long after."

He checked himself. How long had it been since he had spoken *those* words to anyone? Who was there to speak them to, anyway?

"Oh." Ronny narrowed his eyes, glancing away from the portrait, then muttered, "You miss her, Mr. Travis?"

"Oh yes, Ronny. Every day I miss her."

"I know how that is. My daddy packed up his things a few months ago. I don't know where he went. Maybe he died, too? I hope not. I hope not."

"No, Ronny, he didn't die. He's just . . . sometimes folks move on, and it ain't right. Your daddy did wrong to leave. Sometimes we can't control it when a person leaves, like Antoinette there." He pointed at the picture. "They just up and pass away. Don't mean it's okay. You understand?"

"Not right that they're gone," Ronny said as if reciting the point to himself. "Something's not right about it."

"Yes." The old man smiled, let themselves be quiet for a few seconds longer, then asked about the juice.

"Oh yes sir, I'd like some cranberry if you've got it."

They had the juice in the living room, with Mr. Travis settling into his recliner and half forgetting about the black squirrel. By the time Ronny had drained his glass, he was only a quarter of the way through his mug of coffee.

"Well, I don't want my scooter to get stoled," said Ronny, standing up. "But maybe my mom and I will come by for dinner? Or won't you come for dinner, Mr. Travis?"

The old man smiled. "Well, that sounds fine, son."

"Settled then. I'll see you tonight if it's all the same to you! Mom's making steak chops!"

The screen door slammed, and the morning reverted to its quiet self, still only in its midmorning saturation. He could go back to his paper now, back to his coffee, back to the porch where amblers and neighbors walked by as if they had all the time in the world. To all passersby the old house and its old man were unchanged, still in its final stages of decay. But instead Mr. Travis went to the window. He didn't go back to the porch just yet. Ronny picked up the scooter and noticed the squirrel as he was wheeling it off the grass. After some hesitation, he dropped the scooter and picked up the shovel Mr. Travis had lost in his fall, digging a little hole next to the tree. Once finished, he nudged the squirrel into it, filling it in until there was just a neat patch of dirt to commemorate the grave. The child stared at the spot for about a minute, leaning on the shovel, then mounted the scooter and shot off down the avenue while Mr. Travis wondered at the sight and felt his body shake, though not from old age.

The sun shone in bright sadness, and then went obscured by a stint of cloud cover, and the afternoon brought sheets of rain, heavy and light, heavy and light. The newspaper fluttered in the wind and Mr. Travis kept his eyes on the grave of the black squirrel for a long time after.

RAINFALL

J ESSICA leaned on the porch railing of her apartment in Queens. She was tired even though she'd been sleeping all day, lonely because she had talked to no one since the day before, and generally sad, because her life, like many people on that street and in that city, wasn't what she thought it should be. It was raining hard, and the sound made a long *shhhh* in the streets.

Cabs drove by through the puddles, and a couple of people crossed the streets wearing raincoats and holding coffee, hands clasped on their heads. One cab let out a man. He was dressed in a wonderful and expensive sportscoat and carried a briefcase in one hand. There was no telling what he was doing or who he was, and Jessica had little energy to imagine the contents of his life, which was surely much more exciting than her own, and kept watching. The rain poured. Wind blew mist into her eyes, giving her a sudden and fleeting sense of refreshment, and she retreated from the railing.

She went back inside and summoned herself to the sink to wash dishes. She liked the sound of the rain on the roof and against the windowpanes. Rain makes you feel like someone else is there, or that someone should be there, sheltered in place from a world suddenly turned gray and inhospitable. Her apartment was a haven now, only there was no knock on her door, and she remained quite lonely.

She looked up from the sink, turning off the water, letting her thoughts and feelings approach her through the quiet of the flat and the hush of rainfall. Her parents had sent her a letter and it was stuck on the fridge, peeking behind a photo of her little brother's high school graduation photo.

She wasn't sure when she'd go home again.

Her dad had told her last month that she could work for him in the family painting business as a secretary or financial assistant. It was always an option. She thought about it but knew she hadn't come to New York for college just to go back home for a job she could've managed with a high school diploma. She'd been a Communications Major and wanted to be a journalist. It was hard to be such in New York City. But she tried. She wrote opinion pieces about gender and sexuality, poems about singleness and death, and kept a vigilant eye on the streets as if expecting the world's greatest dramas to visit her there.

Her work in a bakery sustained her for the time being. She didn't imagine herself in Queens forever, or even for the next five years, but there she stayed, worked, watched, and hoped for her breakthrough—which all the optimistic quotes on Instagram promised by the day, and which the standard self-help book preached was well on the way. She convinced herself that journalism was her life path, with that uncanny sense of obligation posed on her by her college degree, her letter writing parents in South Carolina, her enthusiastic college friends, her aversion to the ordinary that always compelled her to a blank page that often remained blank after frustrated erasures. She'd really not much to say or write to the world, and she was starting, with great dread and anxiety, to know it.

She did have a neighbor, John, who'd struck up the habit of talking to her. He was a big lovable man from Harlem and had lived in that building for thirty years, and would come over on weekends to make sure all her utilities were working. The plumbing was perfect. The shower worked. Yes, the floorboards creaked but not because they were bad but because they were hard and wooden and very old, older than *him*. And John came to the bakery, too. He walked down the cracked sidewalks, old, retired, lonely, of course. He got a bagel and coffee from Jessica nearly every day, and tipped her well. With all the visits, the tips, and the smiles, though, she was committed to treating him as an acquaintance. He didn't fit the bill for a friend. He was an old man. He was uncouth in his dress and hummed gospel music to himself. He was too proximal and ordinary to be a friend. Friends were the people you study with, go grab a drink with, party with. Friends are your age. John was an old man and a Methodist; she was a young woman and a nominal Episcopalian, and she never used religion as a conversation starter anyway.

She finished the dishes and turned on her TV but didn't sit down to watch. The rain came down harder so streams skipped in the gutters. John walked above her. His floor creaked worse than hers did, but the creaking stopped once he plopped into his recliner and turned his own TV on.

The man in the suit wasn't in the bakery when she went into work that evening. He was nowhere to be found. An old lady sipped coffee by the window with a dachshund laying at her feet, looking prim and pietistic without an audience. Jessica was taking over the shop from Bill, who was a college student and wore beanies and long-sleeved shirts, and always asked her if she was all right working the shift by herself. "Yeah!" she always told him. "Totally fine. Go study." Both Bill and the old lady with the dog left at six fifteen, and the streets were increasingly dark, amplifying the unpleasant orange gleam of the streetlights. It was October, and cold, and Jessica leaned her arms over the glass casing of the counter and blew the hair out of her face. The ovens hummed behind her; she would have to cook donuts that night—very late into the night.

The shop closed at eight p.m., and she got to work baking the donuts. She'd reopen at ten p.m. The ovens blew hot air into her face, the dough was sticky and sweet, and before long powder covered her hands and had accumulated vats of chocolate caking at the rims, sprinkles like confetti on the kitchen counters, and fluorescent light giving it all an unfriendly glare. Cars drove by, paying no mind to the dimly lit interior of the bakery. A few young guys in hoodies and jeans passed by talking about something indistinguishable. Were these young men truly friends, or would they disband after high school? Jessica didn't know why she thought about this; maybe because her own college cohort was so scattered across the United States that it was effort just to pin each of them down geographically. Sarah was off in Chicago doing graphic design. Grace was in Dallas interning with a mega church. Hal was who knows where, probably travelling with refugees and evading capture from totalitarian regimes at every turn. Where were they all tonight? Surely not by themselves in bakeries.

She checked her phone, texted all the friends she was thinking about, and stood watching the blank screen. *Just checking in* wasn't much of a cry for help. Did she need help? Or was this job, this life, the climax of all her past anticipation, the beginning of a straight road that went on for fifty years and then end? This present moment of just scraping by was upended, haunted, by the promise of a long fall in one direction. She bit her lip and went to check on the donuts. Not done yet.

When she opened back up at ten, John promptly ambled in, wearing a grubby green trench coat and fingerless gloves. He said, "Hey there, Jessica! Got any hot fritters?"

"Hi, John. Yes, I've got everything out behind the glass." John came up to the counter and bent low to study his options. His bald head, and wrinkled black skin, and white beard were all covered with raindrops.

"Well, well, well. A fritter it is. And prolly a sausage roll too."

"Okay."

"How're you doing tonight?"

Jessica held the fritter in hand, smelling all the heat and sugar. She wanted the bad coffee to counterbalance the sweetness.

"I'm doing all right," she said, unsure if this was accurate. "How're you, John?"

"Oh, fine. Dandy, really."

"Yeah? What did you do today?"

"Oh, not much. Called my sister. She lives in Atlanta, you know."

"Yeah, I think you told me that."

"And she's doing all right. You know, I haven't been down there in some time. But she's doing all right."

"Well, I'm glad."

"Yes ma'am. Okay. How much do I owe you?"

"Oh." Jessica sighed. "You know what. No charge tonight. You've been giving me a lot of business lately."

"What! Absolutely not, young lady." John dug around in his pockets and unearthed a roll of dollar bills. "Now here. Take it all. I don't need it!"

"This is way too much. This is the opposite of what I was trying to do here," she said.

"Nonsense. Go ahead." She looked closely. He held about twelve dollars in total.

"Won't you let me?" said John.

Jessica smiled, let her shoulders ease, and took the money. "Thank you, John. Thank you."

"All right, then. Ha. All settled. You owe me a cup of coffee in the morning."

He winked and started walking towards the door, nibbling at the fritter. He really did like all the stuff here. "John?" she called.

He stopped, turned.

"You want that cup of coffee tonight?"

He said, why yes, he did in fact; it wasn't *too* late. So, she brought up some chairs and had John sit down, and got the coffee in a paper cup, from which he sipped and gave satisfied sighs, and then he talked. Lord, the man talked. It was like a waterfall of words. Jessica heard Atlanta, death, and struggle. She heard doubt, Harlem, and stress. She heard old age, peace, loneliness. She heard John. It was good material for an article too, chock full of accounts of trouble and pain, change and turmoil.

"Well, you don't want to hear this!" he said after forty-five minutes of her "hearing this." Jessica surprised herself. She really did want to hear this, even as her phone buzzed with notifications. Sarah was doing amazing. Grace was being promoted. Fine then— she sat in an empty bakery with her old man neighbor.

"All right then. All right."

The rain fell hard until about two a.m., and that's when the two friends walked home, Jessica to her flat and John to his, and she heard him walk on the floorboards upstairs, open the bedroom door, and fall upon his bed like a tired man who's happy to be home.

Jessica thought about writing down her conversation with John. It was, after all, a pretty interesting discussion with maybe a moral to be mined somewhere in there. Something about the power of empathic listening and the beauty of relationships in a fragmented age. That's where her mind initially went that night as she took off her cardigan and heated some tea on the stove. But she evaded her laptop and instead listened to the whining of the teapot, arms crossed, phone dead on the counter. It was quiet for the time being, and it was good. Things were all right. She drank the tea and turned in, and both John and Jessica slept soundly through the whole night, with the rain still falling slant against the windows. *Shhh,* said the rainfall.

FENCING

J ULIAN sat in the corner of the Aldridge café, fenced in against the wall, and got his coffee, no cream, and a piece of Texas toast with three containers of butter crowning the plate. He got it every single day and today was no exception. The rain outside went pit pat on his ancient Ford truck, and made streams which pooled at the sewer openings in mucky reservoirs that no one would want to ever step in. There was a Styrofoam cup bobbing along the drainage. As he watched, thinking that he was about to go work in such weather, Jim came over and sat down across from him, wearing his cooking apron and going, "Well Jules you off to work today? In *that?*"

"Yeah, we got to put up a new line up at the Peterson ranch, and Mrs. Peterson there wants a wood picket fence put round her yard."

"Oughta keep you busy!"

"Yup, it will."

"Rain ain't going to stop you?"

"Nah. Question is if Rob will get his butt out of bed and give me a hand." He sipped coffee and shook his head.

"Peterson. You aim to rekindle an old flame?" The old cook laughed and hit Julian's arm across the table.

Julian laughed through his nose. "No siree. Don't get no ideas now. Wasn't much of anything. She's out in Tulsa now."

"Ah," said Jim. "Well, there won't be nothing much going on here today. Closing early since Marcie's got to go get her checkup at two p.m."

"She's got a checkup?"

"Yeah."

"She all right?"

"Yeah, well she's been having some back pains you know, and the arthritis is flaring up, and so, it's just a checkup and an X-ray. We need somebody young to waitress."

"Yup you do."

"We've had a couple gals show interest." Jim looked at Julian like he wanted to add something, but just smiled.

Julian finished his coffee and Jim got up and patted him on the shoulder, heading off to the register to ring up somebody's pancakes. Julian kept the two leftover butter containers and lit a cigarette on his way out the door, the rim of his hat keeping the water off the embers at its end. He started the 1987 Ford truck, an heirloom from his father who was too far gone from Alzheimer's to drive, and stuffed out the cigarette when he felt a headache coming on. There was a half-drunk beer bottle in the bottle holder beneath the radio, which drawled country, barely audible against the rain and static. It smelled like spilt coffee and whiskey since a flask of the stuff once busted in the back seat. His foreman Rob couldn't hold an egg if the world depended on it. The rain lightened up as he pulled out onto 12th and hooked up with Main towards Highway 3, where he sped up and looped around to head out on the eight-mile distance towards Stoneridge. The rain quelled and then got heavy again as he neared the ranch. He got a strange feeling of emptiness, not physical, and hoped Rob would be there to put up the white picket fence while he retreated to take care of the barbed wire in the field. She wouldn't be there. He knew that. He reached for another cigarette and lit it going eighty miles an hour.

By the time he had stepped out of the truck by the Peterson's barn, the rain has dissolved into drizzle. Rob wasn't there yet, but the posts were piled on the ground like matchsticks waiting to be burned. He called Rob and got no answer, called again and snapped the phone shut on the fourth ring. Then he shouldered the metal fence posts and threw them in the back of the Ford next to his barbed wire and wire cutters, destined to work alone.

He worked on fencing all that morning, ramming posts into the ground and winding wire around their nubs. He sweated and grunted and cussed and sighed. The sun came out around eleven and made the muddy field glitter, and the cows came and drank some of the puddles up with pink tongues of silk. One of the fattest ones got knee deep in mud, and Julian watched two of the Peterson ranch hands throw a rope around its neck and pull it out from behind. He remembered helping Mr. Peterson do that once when he was in high school. The cow tossed and moaned and he thought its legs might break, but eventually the animal managed to find sure footing and walk off sopping to better pastures. He coughed, remembering it with a vividness he didn't expect, and wasn't sure he appreciated, and tucked his head down again to do his job.

He finished another forty feet of fencing and left the pile at the end of the progress, eyeing the corner of the field where the trees began and the miniscule town of Stoneridge sputtered its lazy engine. Years go by and nature looks the same, though surely those trees were a bit taller, a bit fuller, a bit more confident in their roots. The smell of manure and mowed grass are the same, and the big white house, perhaps remodeled somewhat on the far end, was the same too. Even the newly poured driveway and the glistening tin shed by the back fence didn't pilfer what it was and always would be: a place that he longed for, missed, and secretly always hoped he'd return to.

He and Emily, Mrs. Peterson's daughter, used to spend time together when they were in high school. But she was out in Tulsa, like he told Jim. She was never meant to stay on the ranch. What might she think of someone fencing it all up, and him doing the fencing? Probably wouldn't be surprised. He never wanted to leave this town. Julian parked the truck in the shale driveway and defended himself from the Golden Retriever, Sammie, who maybe recognized him, and showed as much with a wagging tail and tongue and a joyous pair of brown eyes.

"Hey girl, hey there, girl." He scratched her ears. She toppled and offered her belly, which he obediently rubbed, and then stooped down and let her kiss his rough cheeks. The dog followed him over to the sections of white wood fencing that they'd put under the pecan tree, but now he had work on his mind again, and wanted to get it done quick. Being this close to the house made him feel like he was being watched by unfavorable eyes within, and he shocked himself when he realized he wished he could have Rob there to talk to. Or have Rob there to talk.

It was a domestic picket fence that marked the boundaries of a home, and knew nothing of the callous strands of barbed wire out in the fields. Julian put a finger on a pointed spire of one of the posts. They had set the supporting posts already. All he needed to do was hammer and nail. He started setting up the sections of fencing facing the house, feeling the wind come up from behind and dent his Carhartt jacket at the small of his back. He nailed in the sections to the supporting beams and reached the opening for the gate. The tire swing that hung from the pecan tree wrangled in the wind, like a wounded pinata. He stopped hammering, breathing hard, and looked at the tire. Emily would swing on it with him pushing her, back in the day. Mrs. Peterson always chattered on the phone in the kitchen about how many scholarships Emily received. Mr. Peterson always wrangled in the fields in clouds of dust and , once bringing his hand back mangled. Emily started talking about all the things she wanted to do with her life, how the broad world beckoned. Funny that, to them, the farthest imaginable place was St. Louis. She went there for college and came back a changed woman, channeling her former energy into a sort of reservation that told Julian that she'd seen a thing or two, and had returned to her former landscape in order to cleanse it from itself. Or to become part of it. He hadn't asked her. The rain picked up again and Julian hammered.

He put in the gate and tested its hinges. It swung without a creak and connected to a post with a sliding peg. He put the peg into its metal groove, though the alignment was off so he had to force it a bit, and put the rest of the fence together at a single go.

Now he was inside the fence, facing the prairie, his eyes getting hit with the wind so the tears flowed. By the end of the assembly, he was next to the whirring air conditioner unit. He remembered that Emily liked the white noise of the air conditioner when she was in the house, whether it was cold or not. It helped her sleep, and to dull the sound of hammering when her father was repairing something in the garage, or when her mother was on the phone. Maybe Mrs. Peterson was in her husband's office rooting around for their mutual checkbook, although Julian would assure her that a week of credit was no problem. He could send Rob out to collect the goods and make him listen to Mrs. Peterson detail him on her morning as punishment for missing work.

He walked to his truck to finish the last half of the beer and caught a glance of the gable sticking out of the south side of the house. He finished the bottle and wiped his mouth and saw the pale contours of her face just slightly blurred behind the glass window, streaming with rain.

Had she been watching him the whole time, building fences? She drew back from the window, this specter from Tulsa, while Julian stood with his hand clutching the roof of his truck. It was like it had always been. He was standing on the wrong side of the fence, never inside the protected part, the domestic enclosure that wouldn't let him leave easily. When she didn't come back to the window or open the door, Julian got back into his truck without turning on the ignition. Rob had called him twice and left a message: *Sorry boss. Slept in. Hungover as hell. Sorry.*

Maybe he wouldn't punish Rob by forcing him to talk to Mrs. Peterson. Maybe he could go back the ranch alone again, finish the fence in the field, and enter through the gate he had built to go to the front door himself. Or climb over if the handle was jammed, like handles get sometimes when they're new, unused, with a misplaced groove holding it all together—metal rubs on metal and makes a noise.

VENUS

NSIDE the museum, I find that it's got layers of different galleries, sort of like an onion that's got to be peeled, with an abstract gallery at the core. My mother recommended I visit just for a weekend "jaunt" as a way to clear my head. She goes to a lot of museums hoping to have spiritual experiences and to feel elevated to higher trains of thought, or something along those lines. She likes to do that since the divorce with Dad and all. But for me, a porn addicted 25-year-old, this place is as bad as it gets. Why? The nude art isn't sexy, and the other women in here are so modestly dressed I could cry. Most of them wear glasses and hold notebooks in the crooks of their arms, looking genuinely interested in the Turner impressionism and the Andrew Wyeth depictions of the wintry southwest. They're actually taking notes on this stuff. I can't understand it. What point to the paintings serve? I mean really, why?

A security guard is sipping a cup of coffee and directs an old man to the nearest bathroom. They are both banal and unsexy. Botticelli's *Venus* looks are me imploringly, but her expression tells me she wants to be loved, not bedded. I check Instagram, Reddit, and Twitter, encountering a feed of explicit videos, and then follow the old man to the bathroom where I quietly masturbate in the stall adjacent to his, getting it out of my system and returning with perfect composition to the gallery. Onto the next layer.

"You used to love art museums," my mom told me that morning. "Even wanted to become an artist, as I recall."

"Yeah. Hard to believe."

So why'd I come today? Is that what you're asking? Desperation. Some kind of quiet desperation, an impulse to rekindle a childhood joy that was burning on its final fuse. I don't know why I came, man.

I don't spend much time in the other galleries. One of them has got photos of rusting trucks in fields, an another is full of portraits of sad people standing in various places in an empty house. If I had read the caption I might have discovered that the photographs were trying to illustrate the beauty in ordinary objects, including crap that's been abandoned, and I might have furthermore learned that the portraits of sad people were meant to inspire actual people to look into each other's eyes with depth and compassion from time to time and just sort of be sad together without caring it it's awkward. Well. What do they know? I'm sure *I* don't know.

The photos remind me of Jessica's face, though usually when she comes to mind, I head to the pornos to numb the image out of my head. I guess I still have enough social consciousness to abstain from this escape mechanism and so go ahead and think about her sad eyes and sad, beautiful lips, which come to think of it aren't so different from those of Botticelli's *Venus,* and her hands on her lap and her black sweater that has an orange tulip over the chest. Sad Jessica sitting on a park bench verbally mourning that she doesn't know who I am, decrying my inability to tell her that I don't know who I am either and that my thoughts and feelings, even if existent, aren't interesting enough to be valid. It's what my dad told me, and I guess I believed him. The outer layer of the museum is full of old paintings that are supposed to weigh gold in philosophical reflection. Here, elderly couples ease about in circles and observe the artworks in apparent dedication, although some of them look like they'd rather be home watching TV.

The inner ring, though, is only dimly lit by fluorescent bulbs, and there's just a couple of white dudes in beanies, denim jackets, and old-fashioned mustaches rubbing their chins as they peruse the gallery. I blink, eyes adjusting, smelling something like Clorox wipes and vinegar, and realize that I've come to the end of the road: abstraction. I find one canvas with just a big circle in the center bleeding orange from its bottom hemisphere. It looks like a crying sun. Another one is black with specks of white splattered all over, titled, "Stars." Simple enough.

Towards the end of the gallery there's just a rusty chain sticking out of the wall titled "Bondage," and beside it, a silver box suspended from the ceiling by a cable wire. Makes no freaking sense whatever. Some of it is actually kind of hideous. I find a vial of green liquid holding some kind of floating scroll with cryptic text on it. But for some reason, maybe because I'm tired of standing, I sit down on the bench in front of the "Bondage" chain. Well, I think, here I am with all the freaky stuff that may never see the light of day. I have the same question for the chain as I did with the beautiful classical stuff on the outskirts. What do you *mean*? Bondage doesn't "mean" anything, it seems to say. It just hurts a guy. Maybe the first time you looked at the porn, experienced the pleasure, it felt good, but by the five hundredth time, it feels like slavery, it feels like *this*. Scarily, it starts to feel like nothing.

And now I'm wondering what might happen if Jessica sits down next to me, looking sad and like she wants to understand. "What are you feeling?" she might ask. I point to the chain, the suspended box, the vial, and whisper, "Like this."

Meanwhile, the proximal hipsters say something pseudo about neo-deconstructivism, and I smile sadly to myself. Yeah, that's right—sadly. Jessica is the Venus-girl. I could never get her in my hip pocket like I could with my dopamine phone machine. I never could manage to get her to sleep with me, though lots of other girls did it without a thought. That might be something, you know.

I stand up and head back to the outer layer to give her another chance.

THE BEAVER

IT was sweater weather. University of Oklahoma alumni basketball sweater weather. The birch trees surrounding Jamison
Park were gray, and the mulberries were gray. The Canada
geese, black and white although with an added layer of gray on
top, were pooping gray poop on the sidewalk and gray runners
had to pay attention to avoid getting a poopy gray shoe. Jamison
Lake was quiet and fishless, with a septic fountain gushing water
out in the middle. Families were out. Young moms pushed their
babies in baby carriages and some of their young professional hus-
bands chatted in business tones and with furrowed brows a safe
distance behind them. It was ordinary, you could say. A gray world,
sure, but a dependable world, one that was easy to predict. It was
not summer, and it was not winter, not hot, and not cold. As for
me, I was neither asleep nor awake. I was neither happy nor sad.
Nothing in the slow mode of existence called for sensation. We all
lived numb in the world, which was numb to us, but it wasn't so
bad, honestly. I had my chocolates and mac and cheese and *The
Office* and *Friends* to binge on my TV, and then long spread-out
nights of tossing and turning and long spread-out days of simple
monotony at work at my marketing job.

My daily walks around Jamison Park were more like strolls.
Meanderings. I could afford to put my hands in my pockets and
go easy. But I never really stopped to look at anything either. Most

things are blurry, especially when they're moving. It takes a fierce kind of focus to clarify the figure of a tree or the shape of a dog. Most people don't even try to focus on each other's eyes because that means they would be inclined to feel something that they would probably be more comfortable not feeling. My strolls were casual journeys through a familiar milieu, and I never saw anything weird or alien. I did not believe in aliens.

It was on one of the grayest days there ever was when a runner passed me on the sidewalk wearing orange shorts and silver, sleeveless top. He ran stridently, composed, with an erudite chin and concentrated eye, teeth clamped on a cross necklace and breath coming out in snorts with every step. Maybe he ran for the local college, or maybe he was an amateur devotee. Within a few minutes I could see those pair of shorts flashing orange from across the lake, scattering geese and drawing the attention of some loafers smoking in their Chevys, some of whom were trying to impress their girlfriends in the passenger's seats simply by virtue of owning Chevys. He was still running the pace, set on some invisible goal. Going in circles? He passed me again. This time I removed myself from the walk and pretended to observe the water. I saw the head of a beaver carrying a reed in its mouth. Plip, plop, went the Brooks tennis shoes. The beaver was building a dam where the lake flowed into a creek through the woods. I had never walked through those woods or took much time to understand how a beaver has the ingenuity to build something like that. Or for that matter, what kind of motivation would lead this young man to run around the park with the nimbleness of a Greek Olympic. Was he training for a marathon? A 5k? He lapped me again just as I went back to the sidewalk, not breathing the way it seemed like he should be breathing going at that speed and distance. It all seemed sort of pathetic. Me, just inching along, not even apace with the beaver, who was already building a patio off his flat and probably had plans for a second floor. And the runner, so in shape that the Chevy guys gave up their spots by the water to some Dodge Rams just so they could get their girlfriend to attend to the blast of their engines. Or maybe those Chevys were all in a group and decided it was time for burgers and shakes at Braums. Either way. I started to pick up the pace a little bit. Once I reached Sully Street I would turn off the sidewalk and walk the quarter mile to my house, which overlooks the stone amphitheater and the WPA bridge, built long ago and probably not with saps like me in mind. I pumped my arms. I swung my hips. The runner was not catching up as fast now. In fact, I didn't hear him behind me at all the whole loop around the park. The sun had set behind the trees and a cohort of sparrows dropped low against the water and then up again in retreat. No runner. No more Chevys either. And to my surprise I had started running myself, biting the top of my sweater, imitating the beaver with the reed in its mouth. What was I running for? To what? Maybe I could make plans to build a new patio in the backyard, or train for a race, even if winning my age group was the only chance for esteem. I ended with a sprint, clutching my knees and heaving for breath, heart palpitating as the beaver dove underwater and the runner came to a stop just a few feet away from me.

"You were really going there," he said, with a chuckle. The remark was casual, and he wasn't breathing hard. He wasn't looking for a conversation either, and I was wearing jeans and my University of Oklahoma alumni basketball sweater, the neckband of the cloth still clenched in my mouth with the world of the park returning to its customary gray after an explosion of rare coloration. Even in the dark, though, those orange shorts glowed. The runner stooped to pick up a bottle of Gatorade from underneath a park bench. I couldn't speak I was so out of breath. He took a long, well-deserved draught, and it looked so good, and so easy.

Was I comparing him to a beaver? He wasn't born a runner, probably. He started doing it because, by some magic of uncomfortable practice and joy, he loved it. What did I love? What was I meant to do? The beaver knows, this runner knows. Somehow, they know what they're supposed to do.

The runner walked up the hill to his car, a sleek Dodge charger. He undoubtedly had a good job and a beautiful wife. He undoubtedly treated running, then, as something inconsequential to his central happiness. And so I felt ashamed and stupid. This was just his workout. It was dumb to assume that running constituted his meaning of life. Running in circles as I walked in circles. But the beaver? It was fortifying its home and swam out into the dusky water in search of good mud and good wood. I watched it glide, duck, and build until it slipped inside its home and I realized I hungered, and remained in need of a home, too.

God didn't design the sunsets to be gray, I thought as I walked yet again around the park, alone.

Scraps of Paper

I T's almost dusk and the sun is coming down and makes the yard look like rust. The riding lawn mower is still setting there with the Johnson grass grown well over its blade, and the barbed wire fence beyond it winds in its corroded braids until getting lost in the pile of car parts in the corner of the yard. The mower hasn't been ridden since Papaw dropped it off last summer shouting, "Piece of crap!" and leaving Daddy to wheel the thing into his shop to try and fix it up. He thought it may've just needed a new air filter. He pulled the filter out, getting his hands banked with grease, and put another in from O'Reilley's. It wouldn't re-start, even so. It sputtered black smoke and pooped out in the spot where it's standing now, the foam of the seat ripped up by chicken hawks, where Reynolds the cat is perched with that arrogant pose of his. Not even the cat treats me like a lady around here. I go out the back way and Reynolds jumps down and slithers underneath the fence. The sunset is dipping low, peddling its rays along the watershed where Daddy's new bull is taking a long draught. He won't get that one off for auction—he'll slaughter him next week for us.

Miles my neighbor and fellow high school senior (and best friend, but who's to judge that except for me) sometimes fishes for bass in the shady side of the watershed, and I think I may as well check and see if I can't give him a hard time. Reynolds takes me right to the water, pretty much, and laps up some shallows, getting algae in his whiskers. You know it's hot when a cat pants. The little pink tongue sticks out just a quarter inch above their velvet chins, and then they look at you as if *you're* to blame. Well, Miles isn't there—just some turkey vultures having at the remains of the coyote Daddy shot a couple nights ago. The coyote is mangled, with the brains halfway shot out of its head and its yellow eye teeming with maggots and puss, until a vulture pecks it and makes quick work of the brains too. The vultures don't see me yet. They're busy. Reynolds is observing them with his dumb tongue hanging out even farther, and then starts a casual prowl around the perimeter. He thinks he's a bobcat. Just wait until a real bobcat gets a hold of them. Then he'll know.

The bass are swaying near the surface of the water and eating grasshoppers. The sun is down enough for it to be warm now, not hot. I don't know why Miles isn't here. He was at school today, barely awake of course, with his dumb camo cap pressed over his mullet, twiddling with his pencil but never using it to write. It's always up to me to get him to do his homework, for he's got no mama to get him to do it, and his daddy isn't doing so good, I hear. That's why I figure he should be there by now. What else was there to be doing? Homework? I laugh. The vultures hear the sound and flap themselves up into the bodarks to brood. I go up to take a closer look at the coyote. There won't be nothing but fur and bones in two days. I scrunch my nose and hike up the hill to get a look at the stretch of ash trees and beyond it, Miles's house. From up on the hill, our houses look like scraps of paper. All this stuff littered around that we'll never use. The pop-up trailer is still there, getting moldy as hell, no doubt, just by the dog pens where no dogs live. Miles has a working lawn mower at least, and a tractor too. He'll use that to bushwack the weeds when they get up to six feet tall in the summer. Miles once made this little dock on the watershed. He wanted to put his pontoon boat on it and get out to the middle of the pond where he said he was sure some catfish were bellying around in the mud. He never brought the boat over, though. He just kept on coming up to the top of the hill, where the dead coyote was now, and fished from shore. He liked doing the same thing over and over again, but also liked to build things.

What would I tell him if he did come? Feeling lonely and shut out of my own house, Miles. You done your algebra? I knew you didn't. You wanted to come fishing instead, and maybe meet me here, the girl lost in the field by the watershed. Whatever. You'll figure yourself out one of these days, and things will get better on our respective scraps of paper. He'll ask me if I still want to go to college, to move off to the big city and be fancy and smart like all the important people. I'm going to school here in town, I'll say. Dummy. You can't get rid of *me*. He'll laugh silently, make another cast, his mind clearly on something else.

I stand back next to the stinking coyote. Damn, he stinks. And with the sweaty day it is, sweet with honeysuckle, feels like I'm standing in an upturned grave in a garden. Well. Miles doesn't come every day. He looked pallid today at school, creases under the eyes, a shaking knee, like his brains were oozing out of his ears. With our graduation coming along and all, and just a scrap to live on, maybe he really is doing his homework down there. I give it another ten minutes. Reynolds comes along and tries to woo me over by rubbing his yellow head against my calf. I don't forgive him for glaring at me earlier. But I don't kick him. He sniffs the coyote. The vultures are still watching us in the bodarks, shifting position, their grubby pink heads twitching and blinking. It makes sense that he's not here. Sleeping, probably. But all right. I admit it. It would be nice for him to ask me to the prom that's coming up next month. It's our senior year and he needs to have some fun, not be so alone all the time. He could at least be alone with *me*, next to the watershed, sniffing dead coyote together and watching the mosquitoes land on the water, just to get eaten. He wouldn't even need to ask me in person. I'd be okay if he just left a scrap of paper on the ground, pinned with a lure in the dirt, that read, "Fishin' for a date to take to prom." Something cheesy like that would be okay.

I don't know where he is. I don't wonder. But I bite my lip and pick up Reynolds and get away from the dead coyote, not knowing where to go anymore.

SNOWED IN

I T is a Friday, and I am snowed in. The driveway is a mat of snow undistinguishable from the rest of the yard, and Bucky the idiot beagle treats snowdrifts like they're aliens of world-destructive proportion, yapping at their bases and then ducking for cover in his doghouse. I need to get him inside. Beth is at the window, shivering with a pile of blankets settled on her shoulders, although I'm starting a fire and have the gas stove lit in the kitchen. She sips a cold cup of coffee as I'm blowing on failing embers, a bunch of Santa Claus napkins from Dollar General clutched in my red knuckled hands. What a day. They said there'd be snow, and potentially a power outage, but you don't realize that a power outage is a real nuisance, and even a danger, when the temperature drops to historically low proportions, and you don't have a porch full of firewood like the Andersons up the hill probably do.

It's snowing hard. The napkins produce a green smoke and smells godawful, and Beth coughs and says, "Ugh, that's rough."

"Yeah," I reply, and snuff the flames with some of the cold ashes.

"What are we gonna do? I'm freezing."

I'm freezing too, but only say, "Keep those blankets on your back," and stand up.

Directly in Beth's line of sight, perched on the hill like the lamp of salvation, is the Anderson house. It's a mansion really, with several jutting gables painted a cool blue, gold banded soffit and neat brick layers for walls with a couple of chimneys. It is a hundred yards away but manages to reduce our shabby single floor house to a laughable shed. It's a centennial glory, a real banger of a *casa*. It's been there since before Ardmore even existed and housed generations of a family a mile deep in oil reserves and dirty cash.

We know that everyone who drives down our road ogles at the Anderson house and glances at ours with the thought, *Ouch. They need to tear that down.*

I'd tear it down if I could, trust me. I'd built Beth a glorious castle with a million towers and a bunch of rooms just for clothes. I'd have a brand-new Ford Ranger in the driveway and a bunch of ambling cattle out back just to give some down to earth flavor to the extravagance.

"Get into the kitchen. Warmer there," I tell her.

"Smells like gas in there."

"Well, I can't help that."

"You could if you'd—" but her rebuttal turns into a grumble, and she shuffles to the kitchen. I can see her breath and the forecast in the paper promises three more days of sub-zero temperatures.

I've tried the 1990 Pontiac in the driveway. Dead as a doornail. I've tried calling Gil from work. Beep beep beep. Lord, I even called my mother before my trac phone dies and there's nothing to charge it with. But she can't get up here in a little old Sonata. Who am I kidding? I cough. The Anderson house is probably full of heat, dripping honey hams, cider, green beans, and candy canes. It is almost Christmas, after all.

"Why don't you ask the Andersons for some firewood?" Beth is investigating the pantries, doing inventory. We've got a big bag of beans, some rice, and canned corn. Also some gallons of water, Campbell's Mushroom soup, and a couple boxes of Swiss hot chocolate. What else could we possibly need?

"I might just do that," I mutter, giving up on the task of starting the fire and reaching my fingerless gloves on the coffee table.

"Else we're gonna freeze."

"We won't freeze. This is the twenty-first century. We won't freeze."

Beth once told me she wanted this place because she could at least look out at the bare hill and dream about living in the Anderson house. Ouch. That hurts a tire salesman like me. The least I could've done is stocked up on some snow tires before the snow hit, but we haven't even stocked up on canned pears or peas.

"All right," I say. "I'm going."

"Okay. I'm gonna call mimi while you're gone."

"Your phone's charged?"

Silence.

"Well shit," she says.

I get out of the house quick and lock the door behind me. The cold bites my cheeks and fingers and I can feel it on my eyes, even my teeth and down my throat. I blink back tears as the wind rolls down the hill from the Anderson estate, bringing flurries of ice particles and snow. I clap my hands together, curse, and then feel bad about the situation, and start praying a little bit just for the heck of it. "God," I mutter. "You know I don't pray much; you know I'm a half-ass kind of dude, but . . ." I don't really know what I'm asking Him for, and then I feel bad all over when I realize I only pray when I'm in some sort of pickle, or my stupid ego is on the line like it is now.

The Andersons.

There's Ray, the daddy of the bunch, with his close-cropped gray hair and ancient Stetson hat and leather vest. He wears boots and Levi's jeans and drives the biggest Ram 3500 I've ever seen, and he doesn't get his tires from me. His wife Jennie is all smiles, and their two daughters only come home from college on holidays, and are home now, last I saw.

But now the driveway is clear. No tire marks in the foot of snow. No signs of life at all except the paw prints of a stray cat, which now perches under the gable of the front door and stares at me like I'm some unwelcome ghost. I come up to the gate and rest my hand on the top rail. A surveillance camera glints down on me with a cone of snow on top of it, but who's watching? And if there really is no one home I'll turn right around and go home. It's a winter disaster, so called. They'll understand.

But in the driveway, I stop, remembering something. Behind our house is a clump of birch and cedar trees. They're probably encrusted with ice but I've got a hatchet somewhere deep in the shed in the backyard, and without a second thought, I turn around in my tracks.

I don't go inside the house. I sneak around and duck underneath the bedroom window, where Beth is likely curled up and shivering on the bed. I open the shed door quietly, dislodging the snow that's blocking the rusty tin door, and go scraping around amongst the piles of car junk and tires, looking for the hatchet. It feels like it's getting colder every second. The hatchet is buried in a plastic box beneath a corroded car battery and a pair of rubber gloves, and even though it needs sharpening, I take it and tramp past the barbed wire fence and up the hill. Just on the other side, the cow pond is frozen solid, and the rim of trees make a green and white band around its farthermost edge.

"All right," I mutter to myself. "All right, wood for the fire."

The closest tree is an old birch, scabbed with knobs and bark blisters. I go right for its base. Hack hack hack. The hatchet's blade, it's immediately clear, is dull as a fingernail, and half the time I miss the target so it slices through the top of the snow, making me stumble forward and nearly bust my shin open. But I keep at it and start making little gashes, exposing the tender white and green of the wood so it peels back in little strips. My fingers are numb by now and the snow is getting down in my boots.

God, it's cold. The snow isn't coming down hard, but the clouds are dark and look full of it.

This tree is thicker than I supposed and in a couple minutes I'm panting, hunched with hands on my knees and that old fury of mine bubbling in my bones. Our beagle sniffs the edge of the pond and disconsolately moans into the void.

"C'mon," I mutter, raising the stupid thing way above my head and bringing it down hard. Again. Again. "C'mon, ya son of a bitch! Ya *stupid* tree!" I'm making hardly any progress. I might as well be hitting the tree with a baseball bat, but I keep swinging, maybe out of some inner hysteria that's been hiding beneath the surface all morning, shouting with every pointless collision against the wood so it sounds like a brackish symphony no one would want to listen to. The snow on the branches falls on my bare head and the back of my neck. I bellow.

"C'mon! For Beth, for Beth, damn it!"

The heat rises to my cheeks and water pools at my eyelids. Whack whack whack. There's nothing except a dull indentation in an old birch tree, and soon my arms are too exhausted to do anything except hurl the hatchet into the center of the cow pond where it clatters and slides to a metallic stop. It will sink like a rock once the ice melts.

So, I fall backwards into a drift of snow, heaving for breath, red faced and at a loss of what to do. I can't go back to the Andersons, for some reason. I just can't. Bucky the idiot beagle is staring at me dolefully by the cow pond, perhaps confused that the hatchet in the center of the pond isn't a bone, and beyond our shabby world, a line of smoke rises blue and thick from one of the three chimneys of the Anderson mansion.

So they are home. And we're home too. There you have it. I go back inside, ashamed of myself, standing by the coat rack and wondering where Beth is. Her voice comes from the bedroom. "Did they have any firewood? Kerosine? Lighter fluid? Anything? Did they have anything, baby?"

I bite my lip. I want to be do good by her. I do.

"I haven't gone yet," I say.

SOLO ELK HUNT[1]

RICHARD knew the valley well. When he tramped in Sunday night, the snow cast it in an unfamiliar glaze and mirrored a distracting cascade of sunset colors that had him questioning his memory. He'd come for an elk hunt, to stay in the hunting lodge he'd built with his brother; now he was almost sorry to disturb the peace with his own footprints. But he walked on, shouldering his rifle and hoisting his pack over his hipbones. There would be ample time to look around. Now, he was tired. His hike had started warmer, but all eight miles of it had been punishing. His bones and tendons burned, his mouth was cold and parched. But he'd come here to *feel* something. To encounter some drama. To be alone. This was good pain, he thought, the testing pain that he was looking for. The wind whipped snow over his brow and chilled his upper cheeks and eyes, the only parts of him that weren't swaddled and wrapped.

He was in a mountain basin west of Denver, with scraggly gray rocks slotting the whole valley like solemn teeth. There weren't many trees up here. The elevation allowed for little but rocks, snow, and a bit of moss by the stream that ran down the slope and through the basin. It was a lonely mountain.

---

1. Originally published at *Plough* online on February 19th, 2022.

He soon reached the cabin. One of the windows was cracked and a stair step had collapsed from rot. Somewhere higher up, a wolf gave a resonant howl. Perhaps there was a pack nearby, and maybe that meant a herd of elk.

He grunted with relief when he got in, stamping the snow off his boots. The firewood from last year remained unmolested in the corner, and the scarred table still had his brother's deck of cards in the center as well as Richard's beloved tin camping cup. "Nothing's changed here," he thought. "Nothing will, probably." The cup was rimed with dust and the room smelled of split pinewood, old leather, and cold dirt. Richard stood a moment in the dimness, watching his breath linger in the gray light of the window. He swallowed, noticing the cards on the table a second time, and knelt to start the fire.

One might assume Richard Pellmore was a busy man, always surrounded by other people, and needed the solitude of the valley to come back to himself. But Richard had hardly spoken to anyone in three months. He spent long hours on his own schedule as a sub-contractor installing electrical wires and drywall, sometimes seven days a week. He had found a working groove of solitary living and was half surprised that his life did not feel lonely. He worked, he watched television, he slept. He talked from time to time with his old college roommate, spoke every other month with his stepmother, who could only remember his name and that he was divorced.

"Mary divorced you, did she, Richard?"

"Yes, Maureen."

"Oh. Oh. You were married to her, Richard?"

"Yes, Maureen."

"Oh. Oh. And your brother Taylor got married, didn't he?"

"No, Maureen. No, he died a couple months ago. I'm sorry. Maureen. He died."

He called her because she was lonely. But he was not lonely. He had his job, his gun, and a hunting lodge. He was okay.

The fire grew to a healthy blaze, crackling the dry pine, and Richard put on cowboy beans with bacon. Lord, how good such simple groceries taste in the cold so far from civilization, he thought as he cherished every bite. There was nothing else in the world he needed, he thought, sitting alone at this table set for two with the hot sweet barbecue in his mouth.

"Well, long night ahead," he muttered. "Too late now." And it was late. The moon hung above the basin, an unseeing eye. Richard put down his narrow mat near the banked fire and slept.

The elk trilled early the next morning when it was so cold that even the stars seemed frozen in the sky, snow dots in a range of dark. Richard turned creakily onto his sore shoulder. The elk bugled again. It was close. Richard sat up, listened. There it was again, long, undulating, and piercingly high. He'd always thought that noise could never be imitated by human lips. What an unearthly sound. Alien and gorgeous, the stuff of gigantic beasts made audible to lesser ears.

He focused his eyes on the still-dark window. Nothing stirred in the basin field; all was dim bluish-white, ghosted by starlight and the moon. His heart skipped a beat at the loneliness, a very big loneliness, intensified by expanse, made strange by beauty. Suppose the cabin fell on top of him? Would anyone ever find him? He laughed. Of course no one would ever find him. He liked to think he was in a secret cove, an inlet of the universe. He liked to think he could remain out here forever and the rest of the world would function as always: oblivious to his existence. It was a strangely comforting thought. Maybe he liked it that way. He had the comfort of having no attachments to the world below. He was high up, and free.

A wolf howled. Another followed, with a deeper timbre, and the pack emerged from the sparse hedge of pines at the basin funnel, black-robed and snarling after the lone elk that sprinted a few feet ahead of them. Richard was surprised by how clearly he could see it. The whole procession was probably sixty yards away—near enough to aim and get a shot in, even. He wanted to scare off those wolves and get the elk himself, of course; he could already tell that this one was huge. It turned and its rack swung and bucked, defying death; then it ran on, this lone chariot with no army to help it. The wolves snapped at the bull's heels, trying to jump and latch on to its neck. Richard had to hurry. He grabbed the flashlight, clutching it with his teeth as he put on his wool sweater and outer parka, still wet with melted snow from the day before. The elk rifle stood propped in the corner of the room, already loaded, its silver lever gleaming slightly in the moonlight. "I'll lose it, dammit," he thought, listening to the animals pass. Snatching the gun, he went out with his boots untied and no gloves on.

"Hey!" he screamed. "Hey, get out of here! Get out of here, sons of bitches!" The wolves had stopped the elk and loaded it down with their weight as they jumped, bit, hung. The elk stumbled, got up, shook off two of them, and made an unsuccessful run onto the ice of the stream, falling partway through where it was thin. Richard drew his pistol and fired it into the night. The wolves snarled and ran, dispersing like shadows. The elk lay where it had fallen, gasping. Richard broke into a trot. He fired the pistol twice more. Dawn began to break over the basin, the ice, the stricken animal. The elk was still alive, struggling to stand. Richard shot it in the heart from ten feet away. The elk thrashed, spurting blood, which slowed to an ooze in the snow and water, and died with a long exhalation that produced a cloud of vapor in the morning air.

Richard knelt next to the dead bull. Its blood was heavy-smelling, metallic, somehow in tune with the wintry stars, the brutal cold, the silence. He was a bit disappointed not to have used the rifle. And he wasn't sure he could claim credit for the kill either; the wolves had had it fairly well handled before he arrived. He observed the dead animal quietly for a few moments, admiring its size and the spread of its unbroken antlers. He placed a hand just beneath the wound. The hide was bristly, warm, and taut. The emptied black eye looked at him, and Richard found himself shocked to remember that five minutes before the beast had been alive—fleeing, heart beating, outrunning a pack of wolves. Why was it alone in the last moments of its life? Why was it not safe among its herd? He touched the warm body of the great elk. He didn't want to take his hand away. He hadn't touched a living thing in three months.

He wished he could have touched the great elk when it was alive.

Drive

T was an hour until dusk, and I was alone on a highway in
Wyoming, way out in the middle of nowhere and hauling a
semi-truck full of frozen meals to Seattle. I'd been driving for
thirty-six hours straight. Coffee cups and Monsters littered the
seats, and I had to keep slapping myself in the face to stay awake.
No one else drove on the stretch of road and hadn't been for about
two hours, and usually, I do all right with these long drives. I take
them all the time. It's the job. My hands were shaking, from the
caffeine, I suppose, and I don't want to guess what my face looked
like. I made it a point to never look in a mirror when on the road.
Or off the road, for that matter.

I last stopped in Denver.

There, May called me. She lives in Boulder. So, I drove on to
Boulder, not sure why I wanted to stir up that can of worms again,
but I did it all the same. She was all broken up over the death of
her sister—crying on her couch with her legs folded and her head
buried in a pillow so I couldn't even see her face. I didn't know
what to say, sitting on the edge of the windowsill holding a can of
beer, tired out of my mind. I never knew what to say when we were
together in college.

"You ran off," she said later that night. "You ran off with someone else."

She was right, and I walked out again that night in not so different a way than the first time—with no explanation and no kiss. She didn't want me to kiss her. I wanted to, then didn't want to, then wasn't sure, and so left.

Now I drove and drove into a thick black night trespassed only by my headlights and Denver glimmered impossibly far behind me.

And maybe it was the lack of sleep, or the bad lighting, or if in some bizarre way if it was real, but as I drove on alone, I saw this guy sprinting down the shoulder of the highway wearing a long trench coat and a top hat.

He looked to be running like his life depended on it.

He held something under one arm, but I couldn't tell what it was when I passed him going seventy miles an hour. Well, I didn't know what to think. I didn't think much of it, honestly, and thought I was probably just seeing things. I turned on the radio, listening to country music because it was the first thing that came on, blinking big and slapping myself in the face. I rounded a corner where a sign promised a township in 37 miles. Good. I could get fuel there. But as I kept on driving and as it got darker, I saw the same guy, running the same way with the same package under his arm. This time I slowed way down, rubbed my eyes, and peered in the rearview mirror. Nothing. Not a sight of him behind me. Surely there were weirdos in this part of the country, like there are all over. I see freaks and crazies all the time on this job. One time I saw a man crawling down the highway. There was a woman at a gas station in Nevada who wouldn't stop screaming in the parking lot. People are nuts. They say all sorts of things to you that aren't your problem. They try to cry on your shoulder. And I never know what to do. So I kept on going.

Ten minutes later, there he was again: running, running, running, his coattails bobbing and his black dress shoes kicking up dust. What was he holding, doggone it? Was it a book? The Bible? A compass or radio? A sandwich? I slapped myself hard this time and drank more coffee, and still that little bitty town didn't show up.

The fourth time I saw the man, there was still no one else on the road, but the town lay at the end of a long slope, and a gas station flickered with numerals on its display board. There was this kind of craziness in the way he was sprinting. Like he was running away from something that he couldn't quite beat, though without ever getting tired or giving up. And you know what? I didn't pull into the gas station. Yes, I was on empty. Yes, there wouldn't be another town for two hundred miles, but that dude behind me (in front of me?) had me kind of spooked, and I couldn't stop. I just couldn't stop.

Of course, it only took a few minutes for me to realize what a stupid mistake I'd made. I was just seeing things. Truckers tell you all sorts of crap they see on the road. UFOs, panthers. Naked aliens and talking trees. America tricks you, man, they say. The American desert, all that empty space, where no one ever goes, that no one ever looks at—yeah, that's where all the creepy stuff goes down. I never believe what they say. They're all high on crack or something. Me? I've been ingesting caffeine and that's it, honest to God.

So it wasn't as surprise when my engine died on a stretch of highway flat as a pancake. This is what I deserve, I told myself, and figured I might as well hunker down in my bed in the backseat until morning. The shipment would be late, and I'd have some people to answer to back at the Georgia headquarters, but there wasn't anything for it now. I bedded down in that darkness, in that silence, and got to thinking about Denver, about the girl I didn't kiss goodbye, about everything I didn't ever want to think about. And somehow, my ears ringing with all that American nothingness surrounding me in every direction, I heard the patter of running footsteps.

I'd like to give a survey to everyone in the country to see what they would do in my situation. Stay in and pretend like they didn't hear it or go outside and see who the hell was running towards them. For about thirty seconds, I just stayed in bed, trying to burrow deeper into my pillow, even offering a prayer to my childhood Savior Jesus, but there was no denying it. Pat pat pat. It was getting closer and closer but never seemed to quite reach the truck. The louder it got, the more I started to shake. Plip, plop, plip. The footsteps ground against glass and gravel. It sounded like the guy even slipped once. He sprinted without a gasp or grunt or wheeze.

So, I got up, and with every ounce of courage in me, opened up the passenger door and peered out into the night. The footsteps rang out louder than ever. I couldn't pinpoint where they were coming from, or from which direction. They roared in front the truck, behind it, underneath it, even above me. Were there just one set of feet or ten thousand? Was it one man or a whole freaking army coming after me? Truckers see all sorts of things. One guy told me he saw tribesmen taking down a buffalo over the great plains of eastern Colorado, off I-70. They carried tomahawks, spears, riding horses faster than the wind. It was the first time that whole trip I thought I might die out here, alone, when maybe I could've stayed in Denver. When I could've quit this job I hate and stayed with a woman I maybe love.

I got out of the truck and had the nerve to turn on my flashlight. The light cut through the pitch-black air like a moonbeam and landed right on the running man himself. Who else could it have been? I screamed and started backwards, spraying gravel and trampling a rotted cactus. He didn't do anything. He was running, all right, but stayed in place. His boots churned up dust and gravel and he still carried his package, but the man was immobile, head bowed, breathing hard. It was like he was a robot, a machine with no brakes and with no destination and with no purpose.

"Who are you?" I shouted. He didn't look up or say anything.

"Hey! I'm talking to you!" Still nothing. "Stupid son of a bitch. Who are you?"

I walked up to him and pushed him. He was hard and heavy as a rock, and felt cold to the touch so my fingers tingled like they'd run up against ice. I backed away. If I bent down, I could see his face beneath the brim of his hat. If I dared to get a look at those horrible eyes and pale, sallow cheeks, then maybe I could speak some sense into him, and beg him to stop following me, or making me follow him.

"Please," I whispered. "I get it now. Truckers see all sorts of things. I believe in you, now. What are you carrying? What the *hell* are you carrying?" I debated whether or not to get back in the truck, and decided against it, knowing that I'd just keep hearing those footsteps louder, louder, louder, and go nuts with the uncertainty of who this freak really was. So, I ducked down and peered into his face. The eyes, large, widened, and red around the edges, belonged to a face identical to my own, and stared back at me with an unseeing insanity. The jaws were tight, the lips clamped shut, and he breathed through his nostrils, but his chest wasn't heaving and he didn't have one drop of sweat on that waxed, grotesque image of what I guess was supposed to be me.

I gave a bellow and scrambled away into the ditch. My flashlight went haywire and landed upright in the bushes, but its light fell on the stranger's arm—the one that carried something unknown. Slowly, as if drawn by a lever, the arm raised a red gasoline can, held by fingers that didn't bow with the weight, and a voice that sounded like it came from everywhere and nowhere at the same time, said, "Drive."

BLIND LEADING THE BLIND

Two large and unsmiling men marched Jordan was led up a flight of stairs; they told him nothing except that the session was part of a bigger study, and professionals were watching him. He was not to worry. He would be let out when he needed to be let out.

A fridge sat in the corner of the room, he saw, as he stood trembling and alone in the chamber with the door firmly locked and sealed behind him. He rubbed his hands and checked the thermometer on the wall, chilled and confused by how quiet and cold it was. His life was *never* quiet and cold.

The one window faced east out over the campus. Through it, students walked past each other, goggled and straightjacketed, transparent but luminous, through the trees that lined the sidewalk. So crass, gray, and grating a world.

Jordan sat down in the one of two metal chairs in the room, his legs shaking, and he recounted the day's events: he was wearing his goggles, staring at his modified version of Casey Terrance on his immersive screen, who was letting him edit her—just a little filtering here and there, some dropped cleavage, eyes replete with desire for him and him alone, although of course she had her settings on "open to multiple suitors." They made love virtually. They were both sitting in their dorm rooms after class, a mile apart, but she came to him all the same with the youthful beauty of Guinevere. He came to her anew every today, open armed and beaming.

"Do you want to go down to the lake?" she asked him afterward.

"Yes." His voice rang deep and clear—a man's voice. Hers was the sound of a woman who knows exactly who she is and what she wants—spontaneous, sincere, seductive.

"Good."

"Me too. I want to go with you."

Want. She wanted to go with him.

Next thing, his goggles drowned in static, and the men stood at his door upon the command of the Provost. They were performing a random survey and he'd been selected and this was his room. It was a box with a cutout for a window and sweet and salty snacks on the counter to keep his dopamine imbalance from going crazy. He couldn't remember the last time he'd been without his precious goggles. Generally, students weren't supposed to go without them for more than thirty minutes at a time. They needed to eat, shower, and defecate, but no one wanted to do that for long. They hopped back on their shared universe to quickly forget they actually lived in fleshy cages—and to think anyone used to walk around in them 24/7!

He opened the fridge and found a bottle of water, cold and wet to the touch. Chips and popcorn sat unopened on the counter. A single light above him gleamed white and cruel. He noticed, then, that he smelled oily and rank, that his armpits were rimed with sweat, and that his underpants reeked with semen and urine. Clutching his head, he felt nothing there, and he whimpered, "Let me out of here. Give them back. Give them back. Please give them back."

Casey told him once that past societies didn't have the tech for such a digital Eden as theirs. "They talked to each other in their own bodies," she whispered, her tailored face close to his. "Bodies."

"Absurd," he said.

"Crazy," she said.

"It's hard enough to unplug and have that . . . that *moment . . .*" He struggled to say it. "You know, that *moment* when you take off the goggles and fall asleep. But there's that moment in between."

"God, it's terrible." They laughed, and the mountains they'd simulated echoed with the music of their laughter as if chiming from the mouths of the gods.

"I wish I could afford the dormancy pills that are supposed to ease the transition. Don't feel the shock."

"Yeah. Someday we'll get those. And you can hire bots to feed you, you know."

An hour passed and Jordan sweated and clutched the chair with his teeth gritted. If they were watching him, he didn't know where from. He thrashed his head back and forth so the spittle flung, his eyes bloodred with vessels and rolling back; he slammed his legs on the concrete floor so his shins rattled with pain.

Why am I here? I. Here. His body existed in a particular point in space, and this frightened him. He felt like he was trussed and burning at a heretic's stake.

Another hour passed. He stuck his hand down his pants, wary of hidden cameras, when the door opened and a girl he only barely recognized entered the room wearing a red sweater and athletic shorts. She blinked at the light, wobbled on her flat feet, and had to brush her brown hair out of her eyes to get a view of the stinking, masturbating, yellow toothed boy on the metal chair. Jordan stood up, heart in his throat.

"Jordan?"

Her voice was lower than she'd modified on her portal. Circles trenched her eyes, and she had a round face splotched with acne. She wasn't fat, but she had more weight on her hips and legs than the avatar let on. She was completely, terribly, normal.

"Nyup." He squinted.

"It's Casey. Casey Terrance. They put me in here. I don't know—I don't know why." His voice quailed, and hers seemed to belong to a girl who is always uncertain about what to say next.

He scuttled to the corner of the room, using the chair to cover himself.

"They said it was for a research project," she said. She felt her head, eyes widening.

"You're—taller than I imagined," he said.

She blushed. "Yeah. Well. You're shorter than I imagined."

Jordan burned red. Something in him wanted to punch the wall, punch *her,* scream at the hidden cameras to let them the hell out.

"I've been going insane in here," he said. "This can't be legal. This can't be right!"

"They were having a Oneness Concert tonight," Casey lamented. "Doja Mania was going to be there in the shared space. And we're stuck here." She glanced at him, chewed her lip, then plunged her hand into the bag of popcorn as if all other options were exhausted.

She didn't move like she did in her module settings. She lacked her swaying gait and red lipped smile; the hemispheres of her buttocks and breasts weren't rounded to perfection like they'd both designed them to be.

He tapped his fist on his knee. She bit her lip until it looked like it might bleed. Her fingers too were greasy from popcorn, and they both wondered: *What are we supposed to do?*

He supposed it was innocent that he and Casey had lied to each other in their portals. Yes, Jordan was emaciated and ugly, and she, homely and moonfaced, but where was the harm in it? No one ever got hurt just laying there in bed swirling in a world of pure fiction.

Freedom, freedom, freedom! No body, no space, no time, no limits. Freedom from harm, freedom from love, freedom from life—freedom from absolutely everything.

But now, becoming more aware that she was seeing *him,* (a strange and horrible thing, being seen) Jordan felt naked, attacked, ashamed. He sank against the wall as she crouched in a fetal position behind the fridge, hands over her ears, crimping her wiry hair. Both were acutely ashamed and repulsed and didn't know that they were in any way real, or there, or human.

The Provost and President hunched over the shoulder of a certain world-renowned neuroscientist's monitor, each whispering, "Fascinating, fascinating, fascinating," though they too were goggled up (cradling each other in the nude on a beach in Malibu, in fact) and only halfway there to really care about what was happening.

HIGHER POWER

You don't expect all the machines and wooden boards to suddenly come alive and try to kill you in a modest Home Depot, I bet, but tell that to Tasha Wooding and she may beg to differ. She went there, alone, with the kiddos at home with Amanda the Protestant babysitter, for a simple, ordinary screwdriver. Jordan's helicopter needed a screw put back in it, and he wouldn't be satiated until it was mended. Tasha was more amazed than angry at herself for not having a screwdriver in her whole house, which she scoured and swept—wondering how the heck they had made it three years and four months in this abode without mankind's essential tool. She didn't know. Nothing ever broke on her watch, and no door hinges broke, so maybe the lack of the basic household apparatus was simply an occasion for pride. But at Home Depot, there was no pride. There was only desolation and terror of a primeval sort, dressed up as technologically advanced hardware. To be clear, Tasha Wooding was an ordinary single mother who worked as a dental hygienist at Happy Teeth down on Wayward Avenue, and hadn't had a date with a man since her days with Phil (as in the Philips screwdriver, for context). She knew how to drill teeth out and poke needles into people's mouths, and was attractive enough to gain the attention of her dentist boss Dr. Byopmor, who hailed from the Slavs and had no teeth himself. She loved her three kiddos and considered them the totality of her life's meaning. She was sad most of the time, but distractions helped. Work helped. And she had no past record of hallucinatory experiences. So, going out to get a screwdriver was no hard task—she had never done it before, but what could go wrong? She thought maybe they'd be out and have to go to Lowe's, or check out the Auto Zone on her way home just to see if the car people had any basic screwdrivers in stock. She was competent.

A clean-shaven man of sixty named Harold greeted her as soon as she stepped afoot the marble floors and was confronted with the smell of hardware novelty: fresh wood, rubber products, paint, and chemicals.

"I need a screwdriver," Tasha said, confidently enough.

"Ah! No problem ma'am," said Harold. "Just talk to Zoe. She's that *chica* down yonder and can get you fixed up no problem!"

"Thanks."

But Zoe knew nothing of screwdrivers. She told Tasha through chewing gum and too much eye shadow that screwdrivers were in *Jimmy's* department and that *she* was busy replenishing a certain beige paint to the home décor shelves.

"Okay. Who's Jimmy?"

Zoe let her head roll down aisle five. Jimmy, she saw, was a skeletal college student who by the looks of him probably designed toy trains and Batman figurines in his spare time.

"Excuse me," said Tasha. "I was handed off to you. Looking for screwdrivers."

"Screwdrivers are down aisle eight," the kid said. "They come in all shapes and sizes. Flat head, Milwaukee square drive, megapro multi-bit, Pittsburgh magnetic, T5 Torx, Philips classic, Robertson twelve-set, the Frearson, the Clutch head, etc. etc." (And he actually said "e" "t" and "c") "Now the flathead is a pretty standard screwdriver and is a go to for those customers of ours with pretty basic screwdriver needs, you know . . . we're talkin' tables, chairs and bookshelves, we're talking loose bike parts and etc and etc, we're talkin' all that stuff! Now the Philips is gonna be noticeable by the "t" shape on the screw itself. You're gonna need a Philips for any "t" shaped screws. Let me repeat. Your screwdriving needs will *not* be automatically satisfied if you purchase anything BUT" (finger raised and eye aimed at the floor) "the Philips screwdriver. I hope I make myself a hundred percent clear because you would not BELIEVE all the idiots who come in, buy the wrong thing, and then blame ME that their precious screwdriving needs were not sufficiently met!" Here Jimmy teared up and took out a handkerchief, dabbing his eyes and continuing with feeling, "So you know I try to stay up on it. I make hardware my study. My science. This here is my crib, where I get *down!* I guarantee the transfer of information. I promise our customers will be serviced. I soldier on night and day to remain constantly updated on every screwdriver detail that surfaces on the internet. And let me tell you, you may not think there's much of a Reddit strand on screwdrivers, but you'd be shocked!"

Tasha observed the screwdriver specialist with a knitted brow and wasn't sure whether to praise the fool for his expertise or shut him up with a smack upside the head. But turned out she didn't need to do anything. Jimmy stopped talking and looked absently at a blinking fluorescent light panel above him, muttering to himself, "A bird nest."

It was a screwdriver, nothing special. She expected the choices to be of little consequence. What she didn't expect, and what no person in her right mind would expect, mind you, was for these screwdrivers that Jimmy had so generously summoned to burst out of their plastic bondage and march military style against her, shanks forward. These bad boys actually marched in regiments, jumping off the shelves and forming their phalanxes under the apparent tutelage of a twelve-inch Philips screwdriver hopping around from the top of a service ladder. The Torx and multi-bits and Frearsons all meant serious business and looked particularly equipped, each in their own way, to hail destruction. Tasha blinked. What else was she to do? She laughed and waited to wake up. These trippy dreams haunted her from time to time. Whatever—she could deal with them, although waking up these days in an empty bed was a bit harder as opposed to waking with the body of a lover there, which used to be Phil, like the Philip's screwdriver. But she kept viewing the amassing army at her feet, and now the electric drills were joining in on the march too, whizzing and whirring from behind like trolls banging the battle drums.

"What in the . . ."

"As you see we have many, many options," said Jimmy over the clamor. "Etc!"

"Your denial of your past and all your multilayered trauma tends to haunt you," she remembered Dr. Dennis saying. "This is a good step, coming here. If you keep it all shoved down, well . . . it won't be pretty."

If summoning a heroic knight to the scene was an option, Tasha would have opted for it, but this onlooking Jimmy would have to do. She ran back to his side, wide eyed and pointing to the miniature brigade, but Jimmy's eyes were glazed, still locked on the starling nest on the edge of the florescent lights. By now, the planks of wood from the lumber department apparently decided to join in on the crusade, forming lines at the head of the store and making concerted leaps and bounds like rigid giraffes intent on the kill. Buckets of paint, including Zoe's beige, sloshed in procession down aisle five. Doorknobs rolled furiously. Paintbrushes dipped themselves in red paint and left gruesome trails. Where was Harold? Tasha slapped Jimmy in the face. "Ouchie," he whispered, not moving.

She ran for aisle seven. Nope, because of the paint rollers rolling handles forward towards her on their sheepskin pads. Aisle six? Another failure due to the uproarious collection of screws, which scintillated brightly in the fluorescent light and shouted in unison, "At her boys! At her!"

Tasha was cornered at all angles, a woman about to be stoned for an ambiguous list of crimes she was only half aware of committing. She had taken the step to fetch the screwdriver, hadn't she? All for her poor son's helicopter? Unto no avail! The hardware parts were on a vengeful kind. It was when the first Philip's screwdriver started spinning against the surface of her ankle that she cried to a Higher Power to help her and suddenly a great host of birds and flying squirrels poured in through the vents in the high ceiling, performing nose dives akin to the Red Tails in World War I. What proceeded will surely go down in military history. How did these honorable faunae know that she loved things that breathed, flew, and fought? And how were they so good as to save her from an army of inanimate metals and gears? Gosh, did they let the screwdrivers have it, especially the leading Philips. "You leave the young lady alone, ya hear?" screamed a preeminent flying squirrel with a golden tail as he tackled the Philips and wrested it unconscious to the ground. "Die vainly, you fiends!"

The birds aimed themselves in flocks against the paint buckets and screws, and there were certainly some feathers lost and talons plucked in the ensuing melee, but the victory was swift and pronounced. The vile hardware parts were forced to limp in shame back to their shelves and reassume their posts as members of an infinity of choice intended to taunt poor laywomen like Tasha Wooding.

"Well," said the golden tailed squirrel as Tasha scooted out from underneath a large boxing crate. "You're safe, ma'am. It's our duty to serve and protect and doggone it that's what we aim to do in moments of trial."

"Well . . . thank you," Tasha said with all the birds, which were painted so many natural colors she couldn't even hope to count them all. "I think you've all just saved my life."

"Glad to do it, glad to do it!" they all chirped and chattered. And just as soon as they had come in, they all flew away, leaving the modest Home Depot in its same assortment of chemicals and machines and screwdrivers, with Jimmy the screwdriver extraordinaire still starting idly at the bird's nest.

Tasha, as a plan B, dropped by Philip's house after the Home Depot debacle to borrow a screwdriver. They had a long talk and Philip (as in Philips screwdriver for context) ended up going over to help Jordan with the helicopter himself.

SHOOTING THE SATYR[1]

SUSAN cooked the muffins in the kitchen and Caden sat at the table adjusting the new camera with knitted brow and the first signs of a beer belly toppling like dough through his Coffee Coupe T-Shirt. He was going to take pictures of buffalos and rocks in the corner of the state that day and then send them to a magazine that usually ended up unread on people's glass coffee tables. The magazine, called *Nature OK,* offered to sponsor him, and Caden thought, *Hey, a shot at a career in photography.*

"Blueberry muffins are ready," said Susan.

Click. Tick-tick. There. Lens cap on and camera off, sleeping.

"Awesome." Click-snap, whizz. All set, camera zipped up in the leather bag and ready to go. Caden poured them both mugs of coffee from a softly bubbling Chemex funnel, which looked like it belonged in a laboratory, and checked the Oklahoma City skyline, rued with indigo and azure from the early morning sun, through the window above the sink. Susan arranged her glass mug next to the fresh gallery of muffins, strung her husband's finger through hers, and took a picture of the culinary bliss through her iPhone, screen pressed close against her grinning face with the comingling steam stringing itself up to a vivid white ceiling, like incense. The caption? *Sending him off the right way.*

1. Originally published in *Dappled Things,* Easter 2022, Vol. 17, Issue 2.

Caden smiled at the photo, took a muffin and the coffee and sat on the velvet sofa in front of the coffee table, which was a glass disk that had a copy of *Nature OK*, freshly minted and unopened, laying on its mirrored surface. This was an exciting task. His skills were finally paying off, and incidentally, Caden loved nature. Who didn't?

"Have you ever been out to this place?" Susan asked, joining him on the couch.

"I think Brady and I went out there once and camped a few years ago." Caden mused and shrugged. "We didn't hike much. I hear it has got some dope sights though." His excitement was more nervous, strangely compelled, like the words rolled off his tongue before they registered in his brain. He had never really liked camping, but they camped every month. New Mexico, Colorado, Utah. For the sights, of course, sights made vicarious through shots.

Susan had her brows knitted, legs bunched up beneath her and leaned up against Caden on the couch, studying her iPhone. "Buffalos can charge people," she said, after reading an article. Caden laughed.

"Yeah, I know."

"Oh. People have died."

"Yeah, it happens. I'll be careful."

Susan munched and sipped. Caden nibbled and swallowed.

"Wish I was going."

"You do? Well, guess you could. But I mean, think it's good you're staying for the wedding. It'll mean a lot to her."

Susan nodded, parting from the iPhone and tossing her body sideways to pet Caden's curls beneath his beanie. Caden scrolled through his own morning gallery, numbed and blurred with beauty after the fortieth shot of van lives and wispy faces mingled with the gods of the morning light, slumped back into a curved bow with a sigh. The photo gallery on the table was made of the rich, creamy cover that attracted greasy fingertips. Clean as a sheet.

"Can't wait to get the next issue," said Susan. "We should have a release party or something!"

"Oh, well." Caden laughed. "I mean, my buffalo photos won't take up the whole thing."

"Right, yeah, only like the cover of the magazine, and a twenty photo series! No big deal." Caden picked up the *Nature OK* and thumbed through, gingerly, although muffin grease gelled the corner. "Aw babe!" she said.

"It'll rub off."

There were photos of ranch hands, withered by wind and sun, standing next to oil rigs with their hands at their sides looking out over empty prairie. He did not stay with this image long, and Susan was back on the iPhone. There were dark, shadowy pictures of rivers, glinting silver and yellow in jungle summer. Another one of amber prairie, oceanlike and crowned with a sunset of pink lashes and lavender shoots. His foot tapped. His lips were tightened. He thought, guiltily, what the point was. The image was dead and disabled, with no virtual audience applauding it. How could he know what was good? Left alone with his own judgments, his own solitary views of what he liked and didn't like in a photo, was a boring and unbearable burden. The old medium, although spruced up with gloss and vivid charm to replicate their digital torch bearing competitors, felt obsolete, a waste and an irreversible carbon print. Who would see the buffalo photos? Probably not even Susan would see the buffalo photos. He flipped a page. A Chickasaw woman appeared in mid twirl, her beads and love of the red earth swirled in color and leather, bells exploding on her wise hip and her eyes turned heavenward, not looking at the camera. Caden put the book down, the cover splotched with fingerprints under the sunbeams shooting through the window.

"All right, I think I got everything," he said.

"Yup. So, you'll be back tonight?"

"Yeah, hopefully around eight."

Caden stood up, slung the photo case around his neck. Susan stayed on the couch, thumbs flying like spider legs wrapping up a fly across the screen, biting her lip, and then flinging the thing aside and wrapping herself tenderly around his neck.

"Send photos," she said, and they kissed an airy and insubstantial kiss.

The hour and a half drive to the Wichita Wildlife Refuge was drunk with ambient music from an underground artist named *Flick*. The music added to the sense of adventure, though the intervals between the songs made the silence laden with dread, letting his discordant thoughts invade in fragments and phobias. His brother called and they talked for three minutes and fifty-three seconds. His brother lived in Denver close to the mountains. Close to the heartbeat of life, rivers, the centrifuge. Susan called at the verge of losing service, something about a bridesmaid. Then the music fluttered and shut off, the shadow of a hill covered the tar black road, and Caden dove in the wilderness in an unwelcome quiet.

Farther into the Refuge, longhorns swung their heads of iron in the tall grass and flicked flies with their tails. They lumbered across the road in processions like mourners going to a daily funeral. Caden thought about getting his camera in the backseat, but longhorns were not in the job description. He drove to Elk Mountain without even stopping to watch the prairie dogs. Those photos were already shot and stored somewhere in September of 2015. He planned time only for Elk Mountain, where he hiked alone through this corridor of forest and across a stream inky and quiet like a photo lens, over a ridge and into an open clearing spattered with graphite boulders, cactus, and shrub. Caden stopped to breathe. His Patagonia shorts and Danner boots were a good choice, but he was tired. He blinked, feeling his iPhone press against his thigh in the baggy pocket, feeling it more than he felt the warm wind on his face. The camera, slung over his shoulder, slept in its leather case. He suddenly realized that he would have to actually scout out the buffalo. He sniffed. Sage grass, lichen on rock, shed snakeskins and plump cactus fruit, all melded the breeze, all telling him they could not possibly be adequately photographed no matter how hard he tried. He kept going. The magazine wanted a couple hundred photos to parse through, so he took out the camera, slowing down to an amble as an elderly couple passed him wearing Oakley sunglasses and carrying ski poles. "Hey, how're ya."

"Hey." And they were gone and he was alone again, adjusting the exposure, correcting the lens.

"Buffalo up ahead," the old man called behind his shoulder.

"Oh, wow, thank you!" he said, and picked up the pace through a shadowed portion of trail paved with old white roots and stubbly pines. He stopped at the foot of a boulder and raised the camera to his eye, focusing and zooming on its split center. More sage and golden grass, wrangled with briar. He shifted the focus to a tree and snapped the shot, quickly viewing the screen, brows knitted. He frowned. There was no tree. Maybe it was the exposure. He adjusted and snapped the photo again, confronted with a pale picture of the field beyond the trail, Elk Mountain's blurred image of red orange against blue, the Pear and Apple boulders making teardrops in the corner, but no tree. What he focused on was not in the picture.

"What the hell . . ."

He shot the photo again. No tree. Again. Nothing. He swung around and focused on the boulder. Click. No boulder.

"What!"

He wrestled with dials and buttons and features and apps, unconsciously heading farther down the trail, half tripping on a root. He focused on the moon, a mild dime in the east, and snapped, looking greedily down to find just a slate of blue with a sparrow, blurred and carefree, flitting in the corner. Anything he wanted to capture ended up invisible with its background of tree, sky, rock, and grass staring back at him. And if he focused on the background it came up a black hole of nothing. He shot a branch and reached out to touch it. It chafed his hand, pricking a tender spot at the tip of his index and drawing a speck of blood. He got out of the trees and back to the boulder field, touching the sides of the stones and checking his phone. He snapped a selfie with the iPhone camera, only to find that the place where his head should have been filled in by the snaking trail behind him, vanishing down the hill and into the pool of trees, making his neck look like a fountainhead of nothing. So it wasn't just the camera. Maybe he was just tired and dehydrated. He chugged the Nalgene bottle dry and wiped his mouth, sitting down in the grass and rooting for his granola bars, which he chomped and swallowed, suddenly scared they would taste like dust on his tongue. He clutched the iPhone in one hand and let the camera sag and nestle on a patch of clover, and listened to the silence with his breath held. No one else hiked. The elderly couple, he thought in retrospect, had given him a subtle grin as if to say, "Good luck with shooting *that* satyr, bud."

A bird chirped, and a vulture announced its descent above him, circling some unknown prey, gawking with its yellow omnipresent eye on the wasteland below. Caden blinked, breathed, and opened the iPhone camera again. He focused the lens over a clover, watching the image blur and then sharpen, crisp, real, and incarnate, the white fans of the clover curled out as in prayer. He then tapped the circle, clicked on the photo, and was met with a wormhole sucking in an empty swirl of grass, a marred image of something that might not even have been there in the first place.

They were broken. That was it. In logic class, they learned of probability, the calculus of coincidence, of the arm of Madonna moving a stone finger in Florence—how these things *could* happen, but probably never *would*. Both technological devices, both cutting edge, were broken. Caden shoved the phone into the side pocket of his backpack. "The buffalos," he groaned. He walked aimlessly down the trail, back towards the trees, and stopped, head turned, camera clutched in a white knuckled hand. The buffalo eased up off the ground twenty feet off from him and observed him with eyes of glass. Its crescent horns gave it the impression of a god grazing for souls, and its bulk was comparable to the omnibus of boulders in the grassy field. Caden remembered Susan saying, "They've killed people."

If he was ever going to photograph a magnificent beast, this was it. The door was open for proof. He crouched, middle finger and thumb gingerly working the six-inch lens barrel, focusing on the staring buffalo with the sunshine making an orb of brilliance above its head. He took the picture. The digital portrait included no subject. Just a paste of background, an erasure. "No," he whispered. He was a fool to expect the demand of the moment to fix the machine, but nonetheless, pulled out his phone and took eighteen snaps. All of them empty. He bent low and crab crawled five feet closer, the buffalo sidling. He took another photo and came up empty. No buffalo. Was he seeing things? He dared closer. Flies constellated the buffalo's hide and dried spittle streaked its beard, the brown curls straying like sea creatures between its satyr horns. It lowered its head, scraped a hoof on the ground. "They've killed people."

I know, he thought to himself, and took the picture. *Fool!* A blank blur filled the buffalo space in the image and the buffalo bounded forward in a tuft of dust, agile as a panther, and then rebounded and darted off through the cedar trees, leaving Caden on his back with a streak of blood running down his nose. The camera was broken. Was he dead? No, but his head throbbed, and his teeth felt funny, loose, jarred from his face. Caden checked the camera again, then swept his eyes back and forth along the rim of green cedar, the buffalo head a bobbing frock above the boughs. There was no photo to check. It looked like the bridge of its nose had ransacked the lens cap and smashed the camera into Caden's face, like some violent kiss between nature and man buffered by man's technology. This left nothing but an iPhone, dormant and without service in his Patagonia pocket. "God," he groaned, and meant it half as a prayer. "Oh God." He was alive. That was something.

He took no more photos. The sun set and the mountain put a blue shadow on the trail, mending the sunspots on the forest floor into podge of shade. Caden felt his jaw and nose, winced as he walked. The sounds on either side of him made him jump as he went, faster and faster. A squirrel shot up an elm, pausing on a branch, and ogled him, its privacy disturbed. The water trundled in the gorge beneath him, fallen logs and dross ribbing its banks, fleshed with brush and briar.

He stepped over a newly fallen tree and wondered what he was going to do.

Nature OK would blink at him. Susan would stare at him. She would scroll through the phone, and what if she didn't see what he did? He bit his lip and gulped the rest of the Nalgene bottle. When he was a boy he once donned a ghost cape on Halloween and ran through the woods behind his house, down a trail much like this one, holding a hollow plastic pumpkin bouncing with

Nestle chocolates and Smarties. He was a boyish mist in the darkness, feeling invisible but glowing pale in the moon. It was only when he burst through the backdoor and lost the costume and wolfed the candy down in his father's lap that the mistiness left him and he was a kid again, wriggling on a solid lap of corduroy and brandished up against a wall of assuring tweed, which smelled of polyester and beard resin. The ghost cape lay wrinkled and folded on the floor and his dad kissed his head. What had he wanted to be back then? Not a photographer, that was certain. He liked beetles and birds and mushrooms, all the mulchy, wet, slimy girth of the woods. The beetles and mushrooms he dried and pinned, and he looked at birds without every wanting to kill one. He drew their plumages in his sketchbook, presented them as gifts to his mother on her birthday, and romped through the woods in overalls and an eyepatch hoping the world would celebrate his piracy. In the city and in the internet ether, though, where were the beetle Pinterest boards? It was time to pin the real world through pictures, on to big boy stuff. Caden trotted down the trail over the bridge and past the elderly couple, who were eating sandwiches under an oak tree, hunchbacked and quiet. A staff of Gandalf-like magnitude leaned up next to the old man, and Caden wondered for half a second if they'd put a spell on him.

He threw everything in the passenger seat of the Subaru Forester and flitted out into the open Refuge and home.

When he parked in front of their house in the Paseo district, the avenue was muted by the dark, blobbed with orange light every block and populated with nothing except fallen apricots and cars. Susan stood at the kitchen sink washing their coffee mugs from the morning, visible through the frame of the glass door. Caden got out quietly, neglecting the broken camera and backpack in the seat, and stopped on the porch with his iPhone in his hand. He didn't know what it meant when, raising up the phone with the camera open, her form vanished on the screen, leaving running water and a dark window with the glare of the overhead light eyeing him with inanimate cold.

"Susan!"

She swirled. "Oh, geez, you scared me." He flung the door open.

"Are you okay?" she said.

"Susan, are you there?"

"What are you talking about—Caden, your face!"

"Are you there?"

"What are you *talking* about?"

"I gotta hold you. C'mon, let me hold you!"

"Okay, okay, I will. But–"

"Oh. Oh."

He put her hair down and held her against his chest as the water ran on into the drain, broken nose brushing painfully, wonderfully, against the warmth of her throat. "What happened?"

Caden said nothing. They kept quiet, both phones finally dead in their pockets, the *Nature OK* magazine's pages scuttling in the breeze. All the things he had once pinned down were shimmering in realness over his head, in his arms, bright weighty dishes and cupboards bespeaking glory, the flicking wife's lashes against his sooty throat, a creaking floorboard and a glinting cityscape through the window—all hitting him head on.

A FINER SILENCE THAN BEFORE

A
CROW flew over the construction site on an autumn afternoon when the trees down Sarah's Lane were yellow
and purple. The sky was clear blue, so the autumn trees
burned against it like manifold fires. Apricots lay scattered on the
street, smashed and pitted ornaments sorry to have dropped to
such unfortunate venues. The crow took one from the branches, a
live one, and with the fruit, perched on a tree branch not far from
the head of Vincent Clay the construction worker. Vincent Clay
did not notice the crow. He was standing on the roof, tall as an oak,
putting in a gutter along the gable of the house. There were only
him and couple of buddies from their construction company out
that day, but they weren't talking. They looked down. Hammered,
nailed, drilled, posted. They each knew what they needed to do to
get the job done and so didn't talk. But the crow talked. It ate the
apricot with a curved beak of ebony and cocked its head, wings
fluttering a bit for balance, and cawed. More crows flew over the
construction site, caw-cawing out into the chilly, empty air and
seeming to enjoy the newfound company. Vincent sucked coffee
and watched them gather on the branch of the tall tree, settling
themselves as if for a town hall meeting and observing each other
with their liquid black eyes.

He wondered, as he stooped back down to work, if these
birds were somehow talking to each *other*. Even Manny poked his

up from the scaffolding to see what was going on. A couple of the birds, high up on a spindly branch decorated with just a couple of orange leaves, pecked at each other's heads, and then turned their backs away. Still more flitted from branch to branch as if dissatisfied by the available real estate. Vincent briefly remembered seeing legions of vultures collect themselves in dead trees by the lake when he was a boy. Some mornings, they'd arrange themselves in unholy lines along the lawn and spread their wings for warmth. Vincent would walk down the trail to the lake to look at the beaver dam, just to hear droppings fall and look up to see them all brooding there above him, satanic priests in an inverted cathedral.

He finished that day's work and put his tools in the back of his Ford Ranger as the sun made its early decline and the sky turned light blue and purple along the horizon. The neighborhood they were in was suburban; their construction site was the last house of a quiet cul-de-sac outside of Tulsa. They were almost done.

Manny and William smoked cigarettes outside the fencing, squashing the butts when they were done, telling Vincent they were going to get beers and he could come too if he wanted.

"Been that kind of a week, huh?" said Vincent. It was Friday.

"Yeah, man. For real, man. This week's been gnarly. All the rain. Sheesh," said Manny, resting his forearms on the back of his truck.

"I can't go out tonight," said Vincent. "But thanks. Next time."

"Ah, man. Why not?" said William.

"Aw, you know man. Told Hannah I'd spend the night in with her."

"Oh. Yeah, man, we get that." The two men glanced at each other, unsure of what to say. They once knew Vincent as the talkative one. Vincent used to be the guy doing all the inviting. All he wanted to do was talk about how fantastic his wife Hannah was, and how excited they were to have found a house they liked, and how ecstatic they were to be expecting twins. But now, Vincent watched crows from on top of the roof and sometimes nailed things into walls that didn't need nailing.

So, Manny and William said "have a good weekend, man," getting into their trucks and turning on their radios. Vincent got into his own truck sensing the disconnect and lamented that he was the man who hated vulnerability. He noticed Manny's glances, and knew to interpret them as a disguised question, a plea: *You okay, man?*

As he drove out of the neighborhood and on the highway, he crossed the Arkansas River, a muddy ribbon unraveling itself in an endless spool at the foot of the cityscape. He drank the rest of the coffee from his thermos, tasting grounds, thinking about Hannah. She would be home from her day job as a clerk at Gem Jeweler's and would certainly be tired. Neither one of them would be in much of a mood to talk. What, after all, did they have to talk about? Vincent sometimes spent his days at the construction site rehearsing lines for home. Was he supposed to tell her how many nails he hammered in that day? Was she supposed to be interested in gutters, gables, and crows? He thought about what it was sound like in bed, laying there in the dark, and saying, "I saw a bunch of crows today. They were . . . cawing at each other." And she'd roll over in stupefied silence, brows invisibly knitted, and think he was stupid. Wouldn't she be correct? Everything was stupid now.

They had been married for three years, and had married young, both having grown up in a Baptist church in the outskirts of Tulsa, knowing that God arranged their marriage and intended them to have kids and lots of them. They intended to go forth and multiply without looking back.

But after losing both babies, Vincent tried to recall the divine command to heart and marveled at how easy it can be to feel guilty for something you're not responsible for. In a way, he was responsible. He put the life in her womb and prayed favor over its growth. He blamed himself and she blamed herself, both trying to figure out what in the world God might be punishing them for, or if they were feeling more optimistic, what He was teaching them.

Now, Vincent provided, more or less, and Hanna brought some extra dough with this job at the jewelry shop. And yet they struggled to look at each other; they struggled to talk. Before the miscarriages it was easy enough to sustain their hasty union, and they could afford to be trivial, afford to go to the movies and laugh, afford to *talk*. Now they had to make a concentrated effort to see each other as anything more than roommates sharing in the same desolation. But they were Christians. They didn't believe in getting divorced. They went to work, came home, ate, and slept, and contemplated their own shame in equidistance.

Vincent pulled the truck into the driveway and turned off the ignition, gathering his thermos and backpack and sliding out the door into a cold, quiet yard. The air had that crisp autumnal bite to it, the sky now dipped with purple at its receding edge, and the neighborhood was cusped by the light of streetlamps like it was set on blotting out the stars. Vincent remembered nights like this when he was boy. There would be cider and pumpkins, and one of those effigies made of hay that he and his brother once shot with bows and arrows. There would be the effulgent sycamore trees lining the gravel drive and the wreathes of ducks raiding the quiet corners of the lake. Perhaps he and his father would build a fire together and stare into the embers late into the night after everyone else had gone to bed. There would be that feeling of eternity, like nothing was ever going to change or ever get lost. He and his father never talked much in those moments, but neither did Vincent feel that they needed to. Some people make speeches through their silence, and it can be enough.

Vincent went inside and smelled steam coming from the kitchen. The living room had remained in its customary disarray, a comfortable mess. Hannah sniffed, and her figure passed in and out of view as Vincent set down his things and ran a hand through his hair. She was cooking a quick and easy pasta dish. They'd been doing a lot of that lately. He decided to go to the kitchen before the bedroom and stood a moment in the doorway anticipating her to turn around.

"Hey, I'm home," he said.

She turned around. "Oh, hey," she said, neck craned. "How was your day? I'm just cooking something quick tonight."

"It was good. Yeah. That's fine." He searched for some way to help and reached for the pantry to get a couple of plates.

"Can you wash your hands first?" she asked.

"Oh. Yeah. Yeah."

He took this as a chance to shrug off his work clothes and slip into a pair of loose jeans and a T-shirt. He washed his hands, and by the time he was back, the plates were set on the kitchen table by the window and the pasta swirled with steam at its center. She was setting forks and napkins and sat down with an ankle tucked under her thigh, almost as though she'd intended to eat alone and only incidentally set the table for two. Vincent sat.

"You want to pray?" she said, tossing her hair behind her neck.

"All right. Um. Dear God, we thank you for today, dear God, and we uh, just ask that you bless this food to the nourishment of our bodies, dear God, and that you . . . protect us this weekend . . . ." He hesitated, and added, "And that you would bless Hannah and I's conversation tonight. Amen." Hannah murmured "amen" and let Vincent serve her the pasta.

"How was work today?" Vincent asked.

"It was all right, I guess. Not very busy."

"Right."

"How was work for *you?*"

He shrugged. "It was all right, I guess. Not super busy either. Just finished up the gutters."

"Oh, well, that's good."

"Yeah."

An orange harvest moon peeked over suburbia. Vincent pointed, "Look." Hannah looked, pursed her lips and went, "Hmm," then returned absently to her meal. "You know I saw this crow today." He surprised himself when he said it. Of all the topics of conversation, of all the original things he could've contrived, he chose that dumb crow—although crows, he knew, are brilliant creatures in their own right.

"A crow? I saw one too. In the parking lot eating a French fry," said Hannah. "See them there every day, actually. That supposed to be special?"

"There were tons of them in this tree. It was like they were talking to each other, or something." She nodded.

"Yeah. They're really social creatures, apparently. Super smart, too. They have what they call 'crow's court.'"

"Crow's court?"

"Mm-hmm."

"Like crow church."

"Something like that."

Vincent watched her without appetite for the food. She bit her lip and set her fork down and said with a tone that indicated she had been going crazy all day, "Can we get out of here?"

"What? Out of the house?"

"Yes. Just for tonight. Maybe to the lake at your parents." She put her hands in her face. "I'm sorry."

"No, no, it's okay. Yeah, let's go. Let's go." He paused. "Let's not even finish eating."

"It sucks anyway."

Before he could think about packing anything for the half hour drive, they were in the truck and backing out into the street, Hannah leaning her head against the window and aiming her eyes blankly at the dash. Vincent felt strangely in a hurry. It was going to be a moonless night and the light already dimmed into at atmospheric haze over suburbia. Why did he have to outrun the darkness? Perhaps the darkness would enclose the two of them and package them into true oblivion this time. They would get there and just sit in pitch October black with only a haunting quiet to knead out some frail conversation about the temperature—there would be no talk about what they were doing there, or why they were even married, or if they would ever try to have a child again. He rushed down the highway among slow moving semi-trucks until weaving on the exit towards his old home; they darted on a gravel road and found themselves going forty miles an hour along some country curves sanctioned by elm and oak trees newly bare from a premature freeze. And then they were at the edge of the lake. Hannah sat in the same position with her fingers linked over her stomach, her lips slightly parted like she was ready to talk.

There was just enough light left to see the indentations of trees against the sky, and a vulture flapped down on a branch of a dead post oak overhanging the water. It was alone and it just sat there surveying the lake, extending its wings a couple of times as if to lord its dominion over the whole world. The bird could have looked at Vincent out of the corner of its eye, or maybe it couldn't see the truck at the edge of the water. Perhaps it somehow knew they would be coming. But it was there, with no crows cawing round it and no hammers or cigarettes to distract from its presence.

"Vincent," Hannah whispered, as if suddenly gaining permission to speak. "I feel so alone. I dream about it every night. I pray but I don't hear God. I try to open my mouth but nothing comes out." She started to cry and he started to cry, too, surprising himself, speaking no words—there was no talking at the edge of the lake. But after a few minutes, when they were spent from the weeping and the death bird was gone, stars came out above the water and introduced a finer silence than before, and Hannah said, "Okay. All right. We're here."

A NORMAL CONVERSATION

"Do you know where the restroom is?" she asked him. He was about to sit down and paused, trying to guess the geography of the steakhouse.

"I think . . . it's that way." She walked off down a hall and he sat down, staring at her empty seat and organizing an already organized napkin with his index finger. The first time seeing her was like getting caught in the rain when you think it's going to be sunny all day. The chill of rain drops, the splash of tires turning corners, and there you are. You're stuck without an umbrella or a proper coat, confused about sensations you thought would go surrendered to the bliss of a sunny day. Nothing to shield you from the cold rain except what little of your shirt you can pull over your head.

She was 23 and beautiful, true, like her online profile reported. And her voice chimed cheerily and in what sounded like true inquisition, matching her habit of ending every other sentence with an exclamation mark in her text messages. You can tell a lot about a woman by where she puts her punctuation.

Going up the stairs, led by the hostess, she had marveled on how upscale the place was.

"Wow. This place is really nice."

"Yes. I've been here before. Two or three times, maybe," he said, proud to have such a ready reply.

"Oh really?"

"Yes. But . . . eh, I mean, on my own time. I don't often eat out in such style, you know . . ."

"Haha, yeah, I get that. New York is expensive."

"Yes it is!"

They were quiet all the way to their seats, and it was just awkward enough for her to ask about the bathroom before committing to the booth, where he was in mid squat adjusting his lapels.

And now it was unclear where their evening of conversation would go. He was sitting upright, nodding as the water was poured, collar open three buttons down, rehearsing the major plot points of his life which he had written down in his pocketbook for reference.

She spent five minutes in the restroom and returned with a "sorry about that" and an immediate reach for her freshly filled cup of water, sipping just the rim as he tried to figure out what to do with his hands.

"So, you've been here before?"

"Yes, a couple of times."

"Cool. I really like it. What appetizer should we get, you think?"

"Well, I really like the crab cakes. They're my favorite." He spoke through sighs, like he was being forced to give an academic opinion on the most basic things.

"Oh really?"

"Yes. I always get those. They're really, really good here."

And so they got them. Neither of them took the time to enjoy the crab cakes, even though the cakes were superb. She took small bites and said, "Wow, that's good," while he nodded, his mind searching for a way to start talking about himself.

She mentioned offhandedly how she was glad to finally make this happen. How dating apps are sort of weird but that she was happy it could work out in person.

"I haven't dated in some time, I admit," he said.

"Oh, really? Well, me neither. I realize this is kind of my first time going on a . . . date in the city. I haven't lived here for super long."

"Yeah. I've lived here for a few years now. It's interesting, you know. It's such a big city, so you see and meet so many people, but it can be hard to get to know people at the same time. That's why

I got the dating app. And you know, it's been especially difficult during the pandemic. Getting to know people."

"Oh yeah, I bet." She paused for another sip and nibble of crab cake, perhaps urging him to complement his declaration with a question, but he only pursed his lips, nodding and heaving a little sigh—the perfect invitation for sympathy.

"That sounds hard," she said. "How was that? I can't imagine being here when everything went down."

"Yes, it was kind of crazy, when at first it all shut down, total lockdown, no going out, all the restaurants closed. We went online with our work, which wasn't so bad. I'm an introvert, so not being around people for long periods of time doesn't bother me so much, but after a while, I realized: 'I want to see people!' And that's actually when I got the dating app. Funny."

"Wow, that's, yeah, that makes sense. I bet that was really hard."

"Yes. I'm the kind of person who, as I mentioned, doesn't mind going alone on long stretches at a time, but I realized over the last couple years that I really want someone. Or, want that companionship." Here the waiter intervened and asked them if they would care for any salads before moving onto the entrees. The couple glanced at each other, his brown eyes dripping with nervous energy, and she said, "N-no, I think we're ready to order. I am, at least. Ha!"

"Excellent. What can I get started for you, madam?"

She ordered the filet mignon and roasted Brussel sprouts on the side, handing the menu over like it was covered with something unnatural, and the waiter took it smiling, saying, "Wonderful choice, madam. Thank you." When addressed by the waiter, the man flipped a page of the menu, looking down his nose at his options, and then after a sigh, he said, "I'll have the lamb chops—ah, never mind how expensive! Oh, we'll have two glasses of wine—your Californian red."

"Certainly, sir. A superb selection, I might add."

"Thank you."

"Do you like wine too, ma'am?" The waiter smiled down on her as he scrawled on the pad. She was taken off guard by the question, registering a moment too late that it was addressed to her and not to him. The kindness in this waiter's eyes surprised her. She was surprised that it was kindness that was *true*, painted just as clearly in the ruddy middle-aged glow of his cheeks and his gentle laugh than in his voice. She put her hand on the table as if telling him to stay. Her counterpart, perhaps thinking he could save her from her naivete, said, "Oh I'm sure she does."

The waiter nodded and left while her date grinned at the tablecloth and waited for her to speak again.

"So," she said, drying her lips after another draught of water. "Do you like New York overall?"

"Oh yes. I always wanted to come here for, you know, the opportunity. I love it here. Honestly, just the energy, the art scene, the *food!*" He thrust his fork at the crab cakes and laughed. She laughed too. "Yeah, yeah. Mmhmm. Yeah, I get that."

"But, you know, at the end of the day, like I was saying, I realize I do want something more, felt like something was kind of missing in all that. Especially during the pandemic, I wanted that sense of companionship."

"Mmhmm. Yeah." Her voice remained tender, sweet, like the waiter's. What else was she supposed to do? This was protocol, it was standard. It was normal.

"And I didn't want to make it awkward, this being the first time we're even meeting each other, but I just thought we'd be amiss if we didn't talk about it all, you know?"

"That's sweet. I appreciate that. And yeah, no pressure at all. I don't expect you to lay everything out on the table right now."

"Yes. For me, it's one of those things where I know I can make it on my own. Like, I don't need someone to take care of me, or to do the dishes and the laundry. I think women are equal to men, obviously." Here he paused as if to register how delighted she was at his sexual politics, but found that she still wore the same fixed, interested, nodding expression. "So yeah, it's not that I want someone to be my caretaker or anything. I'm not like that. What I want in a partner is just someone to experience life with, someone who has the same main beliefs, someone who can get on board with my life vision."

"Sure, sure. I get that." She was leaned forward, chest against the edge of the table, kneading her hands in her lap.

"Sorry, I didn't mean to make the conversation so serious all of the sudden."

"No, no, that's okay! It can be hard to know how to navigate these kinds of things, so I appreciate you mentioning it. I'm glad we could meet in person, too. I actually have a couple days off work this coming week, and so am planning on going to Vancouver. Just to get away."

"Yes. I'm glad too. And I don't really know when I'll be able to meet again, honestly. The next couple of weeks are a bit crazy, with midterms coming up and having all those assignments to grade. I hope you understand."

"No, yeah, I get that. Life gets busy and I don't want to pressure you with your time. It's funny, with this Vancouver trip I didn't even have to ask off work from the hospital. It just happened that way."

"Mm. That's what's nice about being a professor. You get all the holidays off. I generally go upstate or to Chicago."

"Oh, Chicago? Is that where you're from?"

"No. I'm from upstate. I have friends in Chicago from college, though."

"Oh, okay. And where did you go to college again?"

"I went to Stevens, in Hoboken."

"Oh, wow. Did you like it there?"

"For the most part. It's competitive. It was hard to get in, but I did, of course, and like to think I've done all right."

"Yeah, it seems so."

Their food came on immaculate platters. Hers was garnished with a dark sauce and his was Lincoln log stacked and dripping in a basted barbecue glaze. Again, she said, "Wow, this looks so good." And it was so good. She began to eat in measured bites, truly impressed, truly gratified. It was so good that she even said, "Wow, this *is so good.*" And she meant it.

He said nothing. He just nodded, scrutinizing the way she cut her steak as if the weight of his future with her depended on her table manners. He chewed disinterestedly, searching for a window of opportunity.

"I am always kind of nervous when I try a new restaurant, wondering if it will be worth it to spend all this money on food," he said.

"Haven't you been here before?" she asked.

"Oh, yes! I just meant in general."

"Oh yeah, I get that."

They finished the rest of their meals in relative silence, and another waiter, young and without a smile, refilled their glasses of water and their wine, which was strong, smoky, red as blood as it swirled in her hand. When the waiter came back to ask about dessert, she took the liberty to say, "I'm so full, but thank you. Or, sorry, do you want anything else?"

He shook his head, dabbing the edges of his lips with the napkin. "No thanks."

"Well, thank you for doing this with me. I really appreciate it."

"Of course. I would really love to see you again. I think you're really . . . really great. Let me know when you get back from your work trip."

"Okay, yeah, sure, I'll do that. And yeah, thanks so much for dinner. That's really sweet of you."

"Not a problem. All right. Great. Sounds good. I am really so—" He muttered more nonsense to no one as they rose from their seats and he paid the bill and, and they went down the same stairs they'd come up.

They had met at the restaurant, and it was somehow already decided that she wouldn't be joining him for tea at his place. It was a cold night and the streets were mostly empty, planted with the towers of the hub of the world's strongest empire, gemmed with apartments of sleeping souls in the city that never slept.

So, she went to the A line stop, and he to the D line stop. She stood waiting for her train to Harlem. A homeless man rummaged through a military duffel bag on the bench a few feet away from her, muttering nonsense to no one, and the few other stragglers on the platform were absorbed in their phones, trying to figure out how to get back to their hotel rooms. But our man, the Stevens graduate, a smart man who had been to the restaurant before and guessed correctly where its bathroom was, triumphantly walked into his train the second he arrived on the platform, which he took as a sign that their first date had gone extremely well and there would be many more to come.

ISLANDS

EREK and Lexi Henry were two hemispheres, sun and moon, who once reflected and refracted each other's energies in a sort of solar dance. Where Lexi was, there Derek was too, prowling the vicinity for intruders. When Derek was sad, so Lexi was sad too. As twins, they shared a loving symbiosis, and the mutual exchange lasted as long as childhood allowed it to last. Now, they were islands. They were not warring islands. They were islands with a connecting bridge long unused.

The Henry family were to spend Christmas week in a cabin together. Mr. Henry was a medical doctor who could afford extravagant vacations. Mrs. Henry considered herself a mother first, a smoker in secret, and a wife third, and now she was trying out knitting as a stand-in hobby for her boredom and anxiety about losing the twins in the fall to the University of Oklahoma. One more Christmas all together, she thought, before Lexi and Derek went off, diverged from the family system, and would never come back the same.

The cabin, then, was Mrs. Henry's suggestion, and Mr. Henry, historically so caught up in his work that he thought little about the family's escapades, simply granted her the credit card and said, "Somewhere quiet." So, northern New Mexico it was. She found the perfect Airbnb—a two story loft style A-frame on the crest of a hill looking out over a mountain basin, and best of all, the forecast promised snow halfway through their scheduled stay. Maybe—just maybe—they would not leave as quickly as they'd arrived.

Lexi and Derek were ambivalent about the trip. Derek had basketball practice, and Lexi's friend Joyce pestered her to join the cheerleaders to Panama Beach for a few days.

"Please," she said. "I'm not a kid anymore. Like, you can't just *tell* me I have to go on family vacation. We don't even go on family vacation in Decembers. We've never done this." Mrs. Henry was knitting what perhaps was originally supposed to be a scarf but was now somewhere between a blanket and a placemat.

"Honey, this might be the last chance we have to all go on a family vacation together. You'd regret it if you didn't come. Halfway to Florida you'd be calling me sobbing."

"I don't want to go."

Deep down they loved each other. Deep down Mrs. Henry knew that letting her go would signal the authenticity of her love. Deep down she knew this trip might force the depths to the surface.

Derek lay low in his room during the conversation, playing Halo Reach with his headset in talking to his best friend, the point guard of the basketball team, Jaden.

"Bro, you didn't even get that rocket launcher."

"Some alien creep following me, dude. Need a sword."

Derek lived in his own universe. To him, his house and that family were ghosts in comparison to the burning fire of his TV monitor. His clothes were stinking and scattered on the ground. His basketball shoes and many socks were clumped in the corner. A polaroid of his ex-girlfriend laughed at him on his nightstand. He missed her deep down. He missed his sister deep down.

And where could Mr. Henry be? From where he sat in his office, door closed and blinds drawn, with a flask of bourbon on a tray next to his chair, he had to remember that he was driving nine hours to New Mexico the next day, and sat pondering what this meant for him. What did it mean? It meant long period of gazing at the highway in front of him with sunglasses on. It meant listening to his wife and daughter bicker about things he didn't care about. It meant Lexi complaining about the obnoxiousness of her mother's complaints, and it meant a rock wall of silence and mutual misunderstanding between himself and his son, who he already could see in the backseat on his phone, headphones on, disregarding the natural majesty glimmering through their heavily tinted Land Rover windows. But deep down he was excited to get away from work. There were fleshy ruts under his eyes. He felt ancient, rusted beyond his age, and remembered once upon a time that he had actually loved the mountains of New Mexico. Deep down he needed to go.

They left the next morning with Mr. Henry at the wheel, the Mrs. in the passenger seat, and the twins conked out asleep, Lexi in the middle row and Derek sprawled with his legs over the seat in the very back. It was quiet. Mrs. Henry was making sure their reservation was still in order, and Mr. Henry took out his sunglasses as the sun became a dazzling quarter in his rearview mirror. The panhandle of Texas, enjoined by the rolling red dirt of Oklahoma, spread out before them as a bleak invitation to something unknown. Mr. Henry noted the frost on the glass.

"How long a drive?" Mrs. Henry asked.

"About six, now."

"Mmm."

"We'll need to get gas soon." Mrs. Henry raised her eyes to examine the landscape as if she was just now aware of its existence. There were no signs indicating townships, only a straight ribbon of interstate and an azure horizon, which to her was a sign of a promised land. She looked back, saw that the kids were asleep, and turned back to the road.

"Do you think they'll go to school together?"

"Oh, probably so," Mr. Henry said. He hadn't given it much thought, but assumed the twins would go off together. They weren't enemies. They used to be joined at the hip, but Derek's dissolution in the netherworld of the Internet and Lexi's concern over her lack of Instagram-worthy friends weakened their bond. But it felt natural that they should go to the same school. Although distanced through the pangs of adolescence, they still seemed destined to share a common path going forward. He wasn't all that worried about them. He had all the money in the world to give them if they got in trouble. In his evaluation, there was nothing to fear except fear itself.

They ate lunch at Chick-Fil-A in Amarillo.

They were quiet in Texas and for most of New Mexico, speaking only when the landscape shifted from flat plains of gray to the rutters of mountains, valleys, and jugular rivers.

They reached their Airbnb when it was still broad daylight, and here, Lexi and Derek emerged from the Rover as in a dream, their iPhones clutched in their hands, regarding the deep December chill, dry with altitude and resinous with pine scent, with narrowed, troubled eyes.

"So cold," said Derek.

You brought your coat, right?" his mother asked.

"Yup. In the suitcase."

"Well, help with the luggage, then," said Mr. Henry. "We'll get inside."

"It is SO cold," said Lexi.

The A-frame was dark and quiet upon their entry. A laminated piece of paper lay on the counter with details for their stay. Derek and Lexi hurried into their room while their parents switched on the lights in the kitchen and explored the place for a thermostat. When they didn't find one, Mr. Henry snatched up a bundle of newspaper, big headlines and all, and almost asked Derek to come out and help him start a fire. But he only looked at his son, visible through the doorway in the corner of his eye, and said nothing.

"I didn't know we were staying in a room together," said Derek, listlessly.

"You bummed you missed practice?" asked Lexi.

He shrugged. "Not really. Coach is pissed, but . . . whatever."

"What do you mean 'whatever?'" Lexi set her duffel on the bed and tossed the phone beside it, tired of the way it felt in her hand.

Derek shrugged again. He was tired of the way the phone felt in his hand, too, but still held it, as it was attached to the cord of his headphones, as it was attached to his own mind in an intractable union. There were near purple half circles under his eyes, akin to his father's.

"I'm not gonna play this year anyway." Lexi blinked as Derek collapsed on the bed on his back, eyes closed.

"You really are checked out, huh," she murmured.

He sighed. "What did you say?" he said after a couple seconds of silence.

And so, the Henry family reached their cabin in northern New Mexico. Their dread pilgrimage was complete on all accounts. There were no school, practices, video games, or Instagram. Mr. Henry had no office to hide in, Derek no console, Lexi no parties. Mrs. Henry still retained her knitting, which laid in an incomprehensible web on the dining room table. They were together for the holiday.

Mr. Henry now scanned the laminated page for a Wi-Fi password. "Don't think there is one," he mused slowly.

"Might do us good!" Mrs. Henry said. "You've got service, don't you?" Mr. Henry pulled out his phone, touching the screen with his index finger only as middle-aged parents do, and sighed through his nose. "Nothing."

"Oh."

Lexi arrived in the kitchen and asked, "What's going on?"

"No service out here, looks like."

She moaned, and sidled to the window. The sun blared in her eyes but she could see a dark mountain standing like a totem in a foundation of blue shadow and the fiery end of a river, flowing east. For a moment she forgot herself, and then said, "Is there Wi-Fi?"

"No Wi-Fi."

Lexi tossed her head back. "Mom, how could you not see that this place didn't have Wi-Fi?"

"I don't know!" Mrs. Henry cried, throwing up her hands. "I just thought—maybe for once we could *talk?* You know? Like, as a family."

Derek ambled in, looking morose, and blinked at the sunlight. "No Wi-Fi?"

"No," said Mrs. Henry adamantly. "No Wi-Fi."

"Oh man," he said. "Seriously? We're here for how long?"

"One whole week," said Lexi. "This vacation is going to feel like a year."

No member of the Henry family could have known about the escaped convict in the area, because they didn't read the news and hated listening to the radio, but he landed at their doorstep, peering in and holding an AR15 rifle, and, thinking no one was inside, barged on in.

Mrs. Henry picked up her purse and flung it in no particular direction, and Mr. Henry jerked his hands up and down so the car keys fell at Lexi's feet. Lexi and Derek both stood openmouthed and frozen as the gunman reeled, shot through the ceiling, and then bellowed, "One sound and I'll blow your heads off!"

He was a tall menace with a receding hairline and a burly Carhartt, and slunk to side like a fox in the headlights. He wore Converse shoes, and this was somehow the most outstanding thing about him. He looked like an overgrown high schooler upset at the freshmen who've crashed the senior party. He glanced at Mr. Henry, then at Derek, and said, "Slide your phones to me. Every one of them. Make a move and I shoot."

Of course, they all did so. He gathered the phones at his feet with a hand still on the gun and put them in his jacket pockets.

"You got a car?" he said. He was looking at Mr. Henry, who nodded slowly.

"Down the hill," he conceded in a voice he didn't recognize.

"Good. Good. Keys. Give me your keys." Mr. Henry's head swiveled. He checked his pockets and turned around to examine the counter.

"Dad," whispered Lexi. He looked at her. "I have them."

"All right, pass 'em on then," said the con, holding his hand out to Lexi. "I was gonna hide out here for a day or two but a new car's better. I ought to thank you."

He gestured with the hand while Lexi stayed still.

"Don't make it hard," said the man. "I'm the one with the gun." He took a step closer, and Lexi stepped back. She said, very quietly, "Please don't hurt us. We're just trying to have a vacation."

"I don't care about your vacation, sexy. Gimme the keys or I'll kill you. I've already killed once today, trust me."

"Oh my God," said Mrs. Henry "Honey, give him the stupid keys."

"We need you to leave," Lexi said, gripping the kitchen counter.

Mr. Henry said sharply, "Lexi, damn it, do it. It's just a car. We'll get another one."

"That's right," said the con. "It's just a car."

Lexi must've done her absolute best to keep her eyes trained on the conman as Derek, newly composed with a sober and cunning gleam in his eyes that was once his childhood trademark expression, slid out of the convict's periphery.

"The keys!" screamed the man. "Now!" Mrs. Henry flinched. Derek grabbed a fire poker in one hand but it rattled when he snatched it from its rack. The convict spun round just as Derek swung the rod upward, screaming, "Touch her and I'll kill you!" But the conman didn't have to touch her. The bridge long gone unused between them flared up like an electric cord, and once the man collapsed broken jawed on the ground, Derek brought the rod against his shins so the bones snapped tartly and the man howled like a wolf, clawing for the rifle. Derek kicked the gun away and, without a second thought, beat the man up and down, mashing bones, pulping the skull, pounding the gullet, stomach, and pelvis. Mr. and Mrs. Henry laid their heads on the ground, whimpering and weeping strange and wordless prayers.

The convict lay as a quiet lump by the time Lexi pulled her brother away, saying, "Enough, enough!" Derek tossed the rod on the ground, face scrunched up crying, and he shouted at his dad, "What are you doing on the floor? What are you doing on the floor?" Mrs. Henry whispered on her hands and knees, "All right, sweetie, we're going to figure this out, we're going to be fine."

Derek held his face in his hands, then hugged his sister, then faced the body on the ground, and sat down on the ground in a pool of another man's blood, breathing shallowly and feeling his chest.

He looked at his father, who didn't look at him.

Mr. Henry stood feebly to his feet, using the counter to help himself up and muttering, "Jesus" to himself over and over. That's all he said. "Jesus, Jesus, Jesus . . ."

They had not been in the cabin for thirty minutes before a dead man lay on their floor, with the twins intertwined by the window and Mr. and Mrs. Henry at a loss of what to do or to say. The twins held each other like they used to when a tornado ripped through town and they had to get inside the storm shelter. There in the darkness, with the dank smell of concrete and old lawn chairs, they realized their own mortality, and that not even their rich father nor their overbearing mother could save them from it.

They held each other. Mr. Henry gasped at the ground. Mrs. Henry stared at the twins, like a seashore longing for two islands that have long departed from the mainland.

"We'll get through this," she said, ashen faced but nodding.

DEVOTION

L ORRIE had been on this drive dozens of times before with her best friend, Carli. The trees were stooped low in their summer curtains and spindles of birds made arcs and parades against a sky of parched blue. It was a dry summer. The fields were cracked and brittle and the cows had to hobble to get to the puddle of water in the middle of their ponds. It was the usual drive. She was with her usual friend. She blinked. The drive was the same as always. *She* was different.

Lorrie had hesitated over the application form two weeks before; the words WORK AT WOODWARD stamped at the top of the page with its familiar gloss of comic sans. She had not told anyone that she was struggling with her faith, not Carli, not her family (definitely not her family), and she had barely admitted it to herself. Three years of the hard sciences that were preached at odds with her evangelical certainty, the kindness of the Buddhist girl from China, and all the people who didn't believe the same things as she did, reduced her to where she was now—brow knitted and parched of answers on her way to what was supposed to be her favorite place in the world.

Dinner at home was hard enough. Her father told her that First Baptist was still interested in her as an intern for the fall. They needed someone who knew the church and understood the value of evangelism and devotion to biblical inerrancy. They all knew her. They liked her a lot. She took the communion that Sunday morning, bowed her head in prayer when Pastor Bill asked them to, and realized she had nothing against her Christianity—she simply had nothing *for* it anymore, was wont of a defense for its truth, and now saw the faces of a congregation as blank orbs that didn't understand the sun they were spinning around.

Carli did not leave the small town of Adler for college. She went straight to the regional school without second thought, chose the kinesiology major she always expected to get, and knew the boy she was going to marry. When Lorrie and Carli were in high school together, they spent a week at Camp Woodward over the summer, and had agreed that, if God's will separated them in college, camp would always bring them back. It wasn't always easy to keep in touch with the distance and busyness of university life. There were seasons when one of the two would go weeks without calling. And when they did finally call, it took a few minutes to clear the cobwebs and remember what had happened since their last conversation. College blends days together until a day and a year start to feel equally long. Over time, especially during junior year, Lorrie responded to Carli's phone calls with a sense of dread. Her parents could be warded off simply by hearing that she was excelling in all her classes. For them, her commitment to Jesus was as obvious and immutable as the color of her hair. It would be a shock and a horror, for instance, if she shaved her head or dyed her hair some outlandish color that suggested a radical shift in politics. Even that would shock. But deconstruction? Doubt? A crisis of faith? No, no, no . . . there was no telling the suffering to be caused by admitting *that*.

Carli, however, had grown up with an opioid addicted mother and a brother who flirted with satanism on the side. Her father lived somewhere south of Dallas. She'd never met him. Lorrie knew all this, of course, and found her drastic story of conversion to Christianity admirable, even enviable. She was there at youth group the day Carli "gave her life to Christ." They cried together, crouched in prayer at the altar, and talked for hours afterward on just how radically the grace of God can shine in on a wounded, sinful soul. Lorrie never managed to pinpoint the instant of her own salvation. Nonetheless, she had counselled Carli through her trauma. Carli had always come to her when her mother hurled abuses and her brother brought drugs and cronies to his room. Sin and Satan hemmed her in with formidable claws, and only Lorrie drew her out into open airs of grace and mercy. Lorrie served as her portal to safety, to goodness, to God. Now Lorrie wondered if Carli could be trusted to return the favor. Her beaming best friend looked great today, glowing with a natural tan and brown hair that bobbed just above her shoulders. She avoided her phone in the cupholder, even when it lit up with Snapchat notifications from Logan. She hummed for Camp Woodward.

Carli cleared her throat as they passed the ten-mile mark and turned down the music. She asked, "Hey are you okay? You've been quiet all drive."

Lorrie looked over, pretending to shake herself out of a nap, and said, "Oh, gosh. Yeah, I'm okay. Just tired!"

"Wait until camp starts. Haha."

"Ugh. I know. I'm excited though. It'll be good!" She rubbed her eyes, staying casual and reiterating how glad she was to be there.

"Whatever happened with . . . what was his name? Tyler?" Carli asked, apparently not quite buying it. Lorrie smiled painfully. Tyler was the boy across the room in organic chemistry. Tall, questionably Spanish, played Lacrosse.

"Oh, yeah. We're kind of putting that on hold for the summer."

"Really? Aw. Seemed like you really liked him."

"I did. Do. But . . . I don't know. I wanted this summer to be a time of just enjoying my last summer at camp."

"You think this will be your last year?"

She paused.

"Yeah. I mean, I'm graduating next year, so . . . I think so. Gotta get an adult job."

"We always say that, though, don't we?" Carli laughed and shook her head. Yes. They did always say that.

One thing Lorrie looked forward to, at least, was the lake and the dock. She and Carli used to read their Bibles there in the mornings and sometimes sneak out of the staff dorms at night to look at the stars. She had never seen so many stars. The quiet of that lake, its still surface like a dial of marvels, reflecting the universe back to itself—there, she thought, there was no question about the deepest essence of reality. There, God's very Spirit assured her of all the answers. There, she needed no answers.

She drummed her fingers on the windowsill and tried not to think.

"I call corner bunk," said Carli.

They turned onto a dirt road and drove through a field pinioned with oil rigs, and upon a distant hill stood Camp Woodward, an assortment of sturdy tin buildings surrounded by forests thick with rattlesnakes and coyote packs and tiny towns barely big enough for the map to chart.

They rolled into camp on that searingly hot May afternoon with the hum of cicadas in the trees and the excitement palpable in the air, like the tittering of a nervous symphony. She felt that dread in her gut and thought, *Oh, God help me.*

It wasn't so bad as she expected, though. Not at first. She felt the usual thrill of seeing familiar faces, of setting up her stuff in the dormitory, joining the preliminary gossip about the crop of newcomers. Julia said there was a boy, Jordan, on staff this summer who was a pothead, but the camp director wanted to give him a chance. In the words of the camp director herself, the grace of God is all about second chances. It's all about giving someone the benefit of the doubt and letting them deal with those doubts safely. The camp director really believed that. She believed in the grace of God. According to Julia, it wasn't even clear if this kid was any kind of evangelical Christian. He was just out of high school and had vague aspirations to be an astronomer. What high school kid wants to be an astronomer? She didn't know how the staff knew so much about him just thirty minutes into the summer. It was clear they hadn't spoken to him and weren't intending to any time soon.

She and Carli sat together during orientation after a dinner of pulled pork and sauerkraut, but disbanded once the worship service started. David, another camp veteran who would undoubtedly hound Lorrie later that evening for the intimate details of her spiritual life, led the music on his guitar while Jeremey the secret heavy metal lover played djembe a couple feet behind him, out of the limelight. Lorrie drifted to the back row. She was always one to separate herself during worship. It used to be because she wanted to be alone with God. Now it was because she wanted no one to see her, and assume that she kept her devotion. The bodies in front of her started to sway, heads started to bow, hands were held abreast in reverence. She realized after the first song that her own arms were crossed, and she was staring at David's baseball cap.

She was tired.

Outside the window, the thin rind of a crescent moon made an almost imperceptible grin against a backdrop of a million stars. *I can see a million stars.* A song in the back of her brain echoed those words, but she couldn't recall the title or the artist. It was something Carli used to sing and hum on their walks in the park. *Can't count 'em, but I can see 'em.* David began song number three. *This is my Father's world . . .*

No one saw her slip out the back door into the balmy night air heavy with the rage of locusts. She barely even noticed herself make the choice to leave, to ramble down the trail of sand and stop short at the edge of the dock to find someone had beat her to it.

It was that pothead Jordan, all right, but he wasn't smoking pot. If the crescent moon showed her correctly, the boy was hugging his knees and staring into the water, motionless, phoneless, the wallop of cosmos hovering above him like a field of questions. He mustn't have heard her come up because she was walking on sand. He didn't move. Jordan was his name. Yes. When they called roll, Jordan was an empty seat.

She said nothing, only held her breath and debated what to do next. Were his shoulders heaving? He was crying quietly, then.

She thought it funny that if Jordan wasn't there, she would be—crying away under the stars she used to adore with a heart of faith. It was like walking up on herself.

She didn't trouble him. Walking up on him might force the boy to compose himself, adopt the stoicism and self-resignation young men like Jordan invariably had, and he'd probably never speak to her again for the shame of being found out.

For a minute, though, she stayed.

After he was done crying, Jordan looked up at the night sky as if a voice had called out to him, quickly and with arrested breath; and she did too, he as the guide and she the follower. They tipped their heads upward in devotion to that old mystique of the universe, like they were drinking some dark wine that suddenly made it obvious of what she needed to do.

She walked back up the hill as soundlessly as she had come and stood back at her place at the back of the worship sanctuary. Carli approached her just as a visiting pastor got up to the podium, head bowed with the word of God weathered and tucked beneath his arm. A good man is hard to find, they say, but suddenly the room seemed full of them.

Carli asked, "Hey, you okay?"

"I don't know. I don't think so." She smiled at her friend. "Do you think . . . can we talk later?"

Carli rubbed Lorrie's back and said, "Of course we can talk. We can talk about anything you need to. Cry, scream, rant. Get it all out there."

On the stem of the horizon above the trees, visible through the black line of sanctuary windows, a storm carrying gracious rains thundered towards them.

KEEP

I.

CALL him John Mark Harrison. Call him the boy who hunted a near legendary mountain lion day after day without sighting it. Call him a boy in love with his childhood sweetheart. Call him a man of God, or a son of a broken earth; wind blew across the river and found the seventeen-year-old boy standing with an axe and wedge in his hard hands.

John Mark Harrison wasn't much good at splitting wood. He aimed too hard, taking too much care with the position of his foot, always searching for the ideal division where the axe met the log. He went down to the chopping block most evenings after coming up empty from the "hunt" for the mountain lion as if rehearsing his future life as a logger. Late November chilled the mountain and the valley, and it still felt like school had just begun—Jade Valley was promised a snowstorm the next day, and up and down its slopes stood a grand and messy assortment of pines. Some were tall and green, others grayed by blight, some charred black by a fire, and many were cut down and rolled up to be taken to a lumber processor in Denver, Colorado. Jade County was dying. Man and nature competed for its demolition as if for a prize.

He wasn't much good at splitting wood. But that night he chose not to aim so careful and split a chunk of dry timber so the two hemispheres toppled on either side of the block, rocked in the dirt, and then lay still like they'd been killed. The sky was darkening quick. His hands burned. The pile of split wood was growing ever higher by the day, unburned. The first taste of tomorrow's front chilled him, filled his nose with cold trees and water. He didn't mind—he loved winter. It was reason to pull his hood over his ears, fasten on his boots, button his outer parka, providing a sense of security against the cold and all it signified. It was best for walks. Best for spotting animals in the woods, best for hunting the infamous mountain lion. He would look avidly for tracks after school the next day, thanks to the snow. Keep Muskogee would try to stop him, claiming he'd get lost out there by himself in such a storm. They almost got lost together in a blizzard years before; this was the only time, however, that John Mark had even seen the mountain lion. He did not exaggerate its eight feet of length. "So come along, Muskogee, if you ain't afraid," John Mark would tell her. He didn't know if she would come along or not. She did her homework. She told him she thought it best if he did the same.

He was excited to see her and her grandfather, Seymour, that night. At least, that's what she called him. Grandfather. His own father usually got home around eleven from the bar and headed up to join his lumber outfit before John Mark even got up for school in the morning, so his own house barely even seemed like his own. It was an empty shell with a couple of beds and a sparse pantry, with no woman in its unheated walls.

He hoped and expected apple cider to be waiting, and for a fire to burn, and a lazy cat to sleep on the couch. They might even have the Christmas tree up and decorated. Usually they decorated it together, all three of them.

Though the trail was already getting dark, he trusted the house's lights to guide him to its small back porch where the old man like to smoke pipe in the evenings and drink coffee in the mornings. He picked up the pace, careful not to lose any of the timber. Seymour always appreciated a fresh load both for the wood burning stove and for his carpentry work. He passed a pair of boulders dressed in brown pine needles and then dipped low to join the river. There it ran slow and shallow over a sheet of dark stone. An elk drank from the opposite bank and raised its rack of antlers with the fall of water dribbling down its gold brown beard. It walked away calmly as if thinking to itself, "It's only John Mark again."

When he reached the house, the porch was empty although the kitchen window glowed yellow and Seymour's figure shifted behind the glass. Their 1955 Ford truck stood in the drive, the chicken wire fence around the garden slumped in its winter doldrums, and the whole place swilled in quiet and winter.

John Mark set the firewood at the base of the stairs and went up. He thought about Keep. She was probably still working on her biology report in her room. That's where she had said she was headed earlier that day after school. Mrs. Johnson had commanded their reports be punctual, eyeing John Mark with her arthritic hands clasped behind her back. That was due soon, he remembered. And it was not as if he didn't enjoy biology. He enjoyed it by being out *in* it, though Keep made a good point he generally failed to admit: "If you love it so much, why do you want to shoot at it?"

He knocked on the door. Keep Muskogee opened it, wearing a loose denim dress and beads in her braided hair. Her eyes widened and she seemed to take in a sharp breath when she saw him standing there, which made John Mark give a cursory glance behind his shoulder and say, "What, see the mountain lion behind me?"

"You'd like that!" she said, smiling and smoothing down her dress. "It's cold." He came into the kitchen to find Seymour sipping coffee and examining a small wooden figurine he'd carved, the chipping and shavings still piled on the table. The light showed it to be the carving of a mountain lion.

"Hello, John!"

"Evening. Got you some more kindling, if you want it."

"Bring it in! Bring it in!"

The woodstove was indeed burning in the corner of the parlor, and though Justus the rust-colored cat was not laying on his back on the couch, he was curled near the crackling grate in perfect contentment. The Christmas tree was not up yet.

"You done your biology yet?" Keep asked.

He had, of course, anticipated the question, but not immediately upon entry; he pretended not to hear and instead looked at Seymour's carving. "It's a big assignment," she added.

Seymour glanced at John Mark, winking through a pair of spectacles and locks of silver hair.

"I'm going to do it tonight," said John Mark. Keep went to the kitchen counter, pouring a cup of coffee and presenting it to him at arm's length. He had known this girl for seven years now, and no one knew him better than she did. But the way she held the cup, eyeing him like a mother might eye a child reaching for a forbidden cookie, she was miles away. She laughed and gave him the coffee, and they went into the living room to accompany the cat by the fire. Seymour's back was facing them, but both knew the old man well enough to know that his whole body was versed and trained in listening and seeing from any direction, and this was always a comfort to them, somehow. John Mark sipped in silence, having chosen to sit on the chest by the window, as Keep curled up on the carpet and gathered the cat into her lap. Seymour went outside and brought in the firewood that John Mark had forgotten and bent down to place one of the splintery blocks into the fire.

"Sorry, sir, I was supposed to get that!"

"Ah, that's all right! Nice to have the fresh air. Can already feel the snow coming on."

Keep and John Mark exchanged glances.

"In fact," the old man grunted, straightening up and pulling up his belt. "I may go out for a bit and have a smoke. There's still a bit of sunlight left for it." He stacked the rest of the wood on the hearth and tousled John Mark's mop of brown hair, then backed out of the kitchen door already cupping a match to his pipe. The wood crackled, collapsed, throwing sparks again so Justus retreated to the couch. John Mark said, "Going out tomorrow to look for tracks if you wanna come."

Keep had rearranged herself in the chair across the room and started to braid her hair.

"It's supposed to snow five feet. Maybe you should wait."

"Or go early in the morning and skip bio."

"You've got to do that report." She was sober about this.

"You're not my mother." John Mark grinned, and prodded the embers with a kindling stick.

"I wish you took it seriously. Who knows?" She shrugged. "Maybe you could even go to college."

Of course, John Mark thought.

"I'm not going to college."

"But you could. That's the point."

"What's the point?"

"What do you mean?"

"You said 'that's the point.' I missed it. I missed the point."

Keep sighed, standing up and going to the kitchen where she ladled herself a cup of cider from a simmering pot.

"Why? Are *you* going to college?" It occurred to John Mark in the past couple of years that she probably would go to college, and that the nearest option for it felt an impossible distance. Of course it made sense for her to leave; she was keen, kind, beautiful, and smart, and it was more obvious now than ever she wanted out of Jade County. They call it Jade for a reason—for its obscurity, its bouts of rolling fog, its numbered days. Keep said nothing, but she spilled cider, the unbraided part of her hair hiding her face and her eyes. He wanted her to come over and curl herself on his lap, kiss him like she had by the river the summer before. But she was still miles away, and not even by her own will. It was like John Mark had drawn a shade between the two of them, and each time he came over chortling and afraid to talk about his fears with her, it deepened and thickened, like snow. John Mark had asked the question glibly, with his trademark chuckle and air of conviviality, but the quiet made him pause, lose the grin, and search unsuccessfully for escape.

"Did you hear me, Muskogee?"

"Yeah."

"Well, what's wrong?"

She wiped off the counter, holding the mug to her chest.

"You know I've been looking at places—I mean, talking to Ms. Felker about colleges." Ms. Felker was Jade High's principle, idealistic enough to note the town's cream of the crop, and accepting enough to know who would never leave the town so long as the lumber company churned its revenue. She often smiled sadly at John Mark in the hallway.

"Yeah," said John Mark. "And you find a place in Denver or something?" He knitted his brows, running through potential locales. "Oklahoma City? Boulder?" A city not impossibly far.

"I—she—told me about a Humanities Scholarship at this school in New York. Where she's from. New York City, I mean."

"Not a biology scholarship?" He said it glibly again, and winced. She returned to her chair, swallowing and adding, "It's a good opportunity. I've talked to Seymour about it, and he can afford to put me through at least a year. And . . . well . . . I applied and got it. Found out yesterday."

"The scholarship?" Now *he* swallowed, teasing his palm with his fingernails, and suddenly longing for a cigarette. But he had to measure the shock and say, "Wow, congrats, Muskogee. Happy but not surprised, as they say. Wow, gee, New York City! The big apple!" He laughed and sipped the coffee, burning his tongue.

"I know it's all real sudden. And it's a bit overwhelming. For me at least."

"I'm sure it is," said John Mark, shrugging. He was always amazed at how good and natural he was at pretending not to care, and this hurt him the most; he drank some more coffee, looking at the weathered rug on the floor, so distilled with loose threads, while Keep studied him with her chestnut eyes, noting his slouched composure, how concerted it all was, and muttered, "All right then," and rose up once again from her chair with no apparent intention of coming back. Justus followed her too slowly to her room and was left pawing at the closed door, while John Mark pawed helplessly at his coffee mug, watching that perfectly split piece of wood blaze with white fire.

He contemplated leaving the way he'd come—through the back door, but knew that Seymour would gently accost him on the porch, having already estimated the damage done in his and Keep's brief exchange. So, he stood, swirling the coffee, and more than ever that night, hated the idea of both leaving and staying. He considered knocking and offering an apology through the door, sorry that he clearly faked his enthusiasm over her decision. But the apology might be another lie. Was he sorry? He felt like a fool for only thinking about her future departure for school as a hypothetical up to that point. He drew out his knife and picked at a tooth, as if this would persuade him that he was not so vulnerable and weak as he felt, that her withdrawal meant nothing to him, and that by heading out the front door he would simply be excusing himself from an ordinary evening without suspect. It was a small thing. It would work itself out. John Mark pocketed the knife and poured the leftover coffee in the sink. He asked himself why he hadn't asked for cider instead. Now he would not sleep all night, most likely. Of course, it wasn't as if he would have slept anyway. He grabbed his rifle, which leaned against the table, and went out the backdoor the same way he'd come in. Here Seymour was puffing lightly on the pipe, still working on the mountain lion carving by light of the kerosene lantern, a Pentecost flame. He smiled, looked up, and arrested the boy with eyes that both attracted and frightened him, and he stood there, gun slung on his shoulder as the first snowflakes started to fall.

"Sir," said John Mark, nodding.

"John. Boy I tell you, this snow will be something else."

"Yes sir."

Seymour cleared his throat. "You all right, son?"

"Well, sure, sir, I suppose."

"Keep told you, I assume? About New York?"

John Mark nodded. "Yeah. She did. Sounds like a great thing, great opportunity . . . I know it's been something she's been aiming for."

"I'm sorry if it's hard news for you to hear, son," said Seymour. "If it's as hard as I'm supposing, know that that makes two of us." John Mark didn't reply. He was ashamed of himself, had no defense, no recourse but to agree. Yes, it was hard.

"I've lived in Jade almost all my life, and have been deeply blessed by it, but I always felt like somewhat of a failure, you know," the old man went on. John Mark frowned. A failure? "It's not fair. That is, for you and Keep. Having no true set of parents to call your own. I'm sorry for that, son."

"Yes sir. You've been real good to me, though, sir, honest." He wanted to say the old man was like a father to him, but didn't know how.

"Well. You're a fine young man. Among the finest. You've got such life and spirit and love. Don't let none tell you different. But you know, there's a time in every man's life when he's got to accept what he can't change." The old man sighed. "Yes, John, there are things we can't control, and you've got to let it be." He chuckled and shrugged. "Got to let it be."

The trail was dark when John Mark set foot on it, but halfway home, glowed with the first deposit of snowfall. He stopped in the middle of the woods, waiting, watching, eyes stinging with tears. His own house lay dark and unlived in up ahead, and a home of warmth and banishment gleamed its last vestiges behind him. He controlled nothing, indeed, and gripped his rifle with a weight accruing like snowdrifts on his shoulders.

He turned off the worn path.

Yes, there was enough visibility to spot a mountain lion. Enough will in his heart to try to control what he couldn't, to wrangle the monster of the mountain into submission.

The trees were sleeping giants, the mountain their wounded mother, and the house behind him went dark too as the old man travelled to each room, securing his fortress, making sure the front door was locked and that Keep was safe inside.

II.

WHEN Keep woke up the morning after she told John Mark about New York, the cold ate at her through her covers. The wood floor flashed with cold as she stepped on it, and the window above her bed iced her fingers when she touched its glass. The flakes sputtered down in kaleidoscopic glory, and she rubbed her eyes, collecting herself, remembering what had happened the night before. The house stewed with silence and the occasional sigh of its old foundation, but she knew Seymour was awake. He got up and five and she got up at six, as if he took it upon himself to scope out the world before her daily immersion in it. She put on a gray hoodie and jeans, a brown stocking cap and loafers, then went into the living room. Lord, the snow. Piles upon piles dimpled the back yard. It inched up the window with white fingers, begging to be let in. But the woodstove roared, thanks to John Mark's firewood, and the old man sat at the kitchen table again, hunched over something meticulous.

"You still have school, tragically," he said.

"Yeah, I figured."

"Good morning."

"Morning." She put a hand on his shoulder and looked out the window. Seymour was staining the mountain lion figurine a shade of light brown.

"That's amazing," said Keep, sipping coffee and leaning against the counter.

He smiled, said, "Why, thank you."

She put her nose to the mug. Six fifteen, a.m. John Mark may still be sleeping, or maybe he waded through the snow clutching that stupid gun of his with unwavering resolve. She knew one thing. He would not be at school that day.

"John Mark left quicker than I suspected he would last night," said Seymour.

"He had to do his bio homework." She bit her lip at this reply.

"He didn't take the news all that well, I wager."

"Did you talk to him?"

"On the porch, yes. For just a moment."

"It's not like I'm never coming back. It isn't goodbye."

Seymour nodded. "He's never liked change. I know that much. He's like me." He set the carving down and studied it, as though the mountain lion produced in him a host of new insights.

"I'll drive you today," he said.

"No, no. That's okay. I want to walk."

The half hour passed without her eating breakfast, though Seymour offered her oats with apples. She couldn't eat. Her stomach felt small, restricted, barely hospitable to the coffee. They talked no more about John Mark and Keep was grateful that her grandfather didn't press the issue. He seemed to know everything already, and yet assumed nothing; he finished the carving and set it up on the windowsill.

"It's beautiful," Keep said.

"Nothing compared to the actual beast," he whispered.

She walked to school with her parka fastened under her chin and the biology report tucked under her arm. It was a report about the pine beetle that was eating up the trees in the region. Keep's research agreed with the consensus: if the beetle wasn't stopped, Smith and Sophe Lumber would have to move its projects farther down the valley, or else shut down altogether. But this was only for biology. It only reported the facts. The beetle was on the move, graying the mountain slopes as it went like a slow curtain of time.

She wondered about the people who spent their whole lives in Jade. People like Seymour. They just never left. Even when the town shrank, the lumber industry took blows from the blight— they stayed. Why? How? How is it possible to live in a place you know is dying? New York, she thought, is always renewing itself from within by heralding new prospects into its midst—people like her who wanted to move there for school, work, business. And yet did people *live* there? She wasn't sure how one could live in a place that was always artificially invigorated by new houses, new people, new skyscrapers, new *trends*, while fluxes of people washed in and out as temporary as an ocean tide. Keep shivered. The street was empty and John Mark failed to walk out of the diner with a cup of coffee on her way past.

He did not see leaving the town even as a remote option. Did the condescending neglect of Ms. Felker do him in? It wasn't as though the town was a prison. Driven by a dying lumber industry, yes, and one that demanded its full share of workers, but where was the law commanding fealty? Of course, she could not imagine the likes of John Mark wandering around New York City. Or even

Denver, for that matter. She had doubts enough about her own sojourn to the American Rome. She owned no images of the place apart from the pictures in magazines and books. She imagined black and white photos studded with buildings, blue collared men resting on construction poles a thousand feet high, great bridges and celebrities, wine, coffee, and music on every corner. She went to Denver twice with Seymour and thought it was all right. So this was where at the trees went, she had thought. To Denver. To build all of *this*.

Keep pursed her lips. She'd never seen John Mark cry and did not know if she wanted to. She wasn't sure *what* she wanted from him. Happiness, sure—happiness *for* her, certainly. His beaming smile could not always be trusted. Did she prefer him to cry and beg her not to leave? "I won't leave forever," she said to herself as she arrived at the doors of the high school. "I'll come back, or you'll come to me, and we'll make it work. I promise." That's what she hated. She hated the inability to truly make such a promise. She told herself at age fifteen that if she could leave this town and do something better with her life than stay housed and holed, she would. She told herself at age seventeen that such a commitment would be irredeemably complicated by the boy with ruddy cheeks and a brown mop for a head of hair, the boy with that stupid rifle, the boy who wanted so intensely to be a man.

The cement glaze of the hallways reminded her of an asylum that morning, and it didn't help that one of the florescent bulbs flickered at the helm of the biology classroom. She turned in the report and sat quietly throughout her classes, noting how no one asked about John Mark because he was gone at least once a week.

"Keep? You all right, honey?" It was Ms. Felker pouring herself coffee in the break room while Keep settled down for work study at the end of the day.

"Oh. Yes ma'am. Doing all right."

"I bet Seymour was glad to hear the news."

News? She'd almost forgotten.

"Oh yes! He's real proud. Of course, he's always supportive."

"It's nice to have a guardian like that."

"Yes."

"So are you excited?" She may have really been saying, "So you made it to the threshold. You're welcome! We'll see if you get any farther than I did."

"Yes, I'm excited. Nervous, too."

"You're going to do great." Ms. Felker looked up in between packs of sugar, her round face plump and rouged, her wide blue eyes always open a bit too wide. She put a lot of creamer in her coffee, too, so the liquid became light brown and lost its steam. John Mark and Seymour liked theirs black. Keep opened a planner and glanced over the month of December as Ms. Felker tested her drink and walked into her office, leaving the door open. Christmas break was a week away. Felker cleared her throat, chuckled in a high-pitched voice at something she probably read in the paper, and then clacked away at her electric typewriter. She was writing a novel in there, apparently. Something about a dysfunctional family that was more autobiography than fiction. But it was set in New York, the place she would go back to if she could. *And why couldn't she?* Keep asked herself.

The bell rang as Keep doodled in the planner and she left the school building quick without telling Felker. She was headed straight to Church Avenue out of some instinct, perhaps primordial, maybe providential. But she hurried.

She ran.

John Mark's house was dark when she arrived on Church Avenue. There were no footprints in the yard. The garage door gaped and the front door itself stood slightly askew. Keep tightened her parka and her gloves. The chop block down the hill was unoccupied, the stump of wood almost buried. No footprints. She bit her lip and thought about taking the trail to the woods back home to see if he was there. No, he wasn't there. Why would he be there? She walked farther into the trees, not yet calling his name, listening for the crack of his rifle or the sound of his muttering voice talking to himself. He used to shoot snowdrifts in the woods and called this bona fide hunting when he was younger. He used to only go for squirrels before he knew anything bigger lurked on the mountain. She used to go with him all the time.

She tramped through the snow as it got darker, and the wind turned the snow drifts into brambles, and the blanket of snow cocooned the forest in wreathes of cotton and cloud. She whispered his name. She whispered it again. She didn't know how she was going to say goodbye when the time came. "John Mark. John Mark!" She crossed the bridge of stones over the river, a bridge they crossed together thousands of times. She hesitated on one of the bigger boulders hedging the mountainside bank and scanned the river up and down. For a second, she appreciated the beauty of Jade County, Colorado, and this valley—her home. On occasion it felt insane to leave such a sanctum. Then she looked down.

John Mark lay crimped in the shallows with his upper body in a snowbank and his legs submerged, unmoving and blue. Keep screamed—the boy's head bled on one side, and in the snow behind him ran a thread of animal tracks, leading upward. A boot was missing on his left foot as if some monster had ripped it off; or maybe used it to drag the boy in to safety.

III.

John Mark stayed in the hospital in Reston Way twenty miles down the road, where after six days he stared at the ceiling and didn't know what was happening, and then was laid in the spare bedroom at the Muskogee house; here he opened his eyes on Christmas Eve with a pool of sun gathered on the blankets. Keep sat on the floor flipping through a magazine. Seymour read by the window, his pipe hanging unlit from his mouth. He wondered where his father was.

Christmas Eve. Snow still lay in piles and wind beaten drifts on the ground. Keep still planned on college. Of course. She needed to leave. Seymour had finished the mountain lion carving, and it gleamed in a golden ream of light on the nightstand beside his head.

Keep said, "Do you think he hears us?"

"Probably not," said Seymour. "But he'll wake up soon. Doctor said he would."

They said nothing for a couple of minutes. John Mark felt Keep eyes on his motionless form, watching his chest rise and fall, waiting for his cheeks to regain their ruddiness.

"Seymour," she whispered.

"Yes, dear?"

"How am I supposed to leave?"

The old man put down his book. He was nearing the end of *Don Quixote,* whose worn and weathered pages suggested that he read it every year.

"You leave by loving what you've left," he said after some hesitation. "You leave, perhaps, *so* you can love what you've left. And when you've been gone for a long time, when you've learned more about the big world, about culture, science, politics, literature, the great empires, the philosophies that have shaped mankind, you'll know how to come back. I don't know what coming back looks like. Don't rush the flight home, and don't suppose coming back means coming back here. It won't be the same."

"I love John Mark."

"I know you do."

"And he loves me."

"That makes two of us."

"I'm leaving everything I love. Am I insane?"

"Remember the myth of black and white?"

"Yeah. I know."

John Mark rolled over, closed his eyes, and slept.

Early the next morning, he put on some of Seymour's clothes that were draped over a rocking chair and slipped outside the back way. He picked up his .22 rifle, which leaned in the corner of the parlor, gathering dust and light, and slung it round his shoulder.

His last memory of the woods felt like a thousand years ago, and the future, for the moment, seemed impossible. The moment burned with realness, demanded his every ounce of attention as it coaxed him with cold, furling with the vapor of his breath as if transforming it into incense plumes.

He looked over that morning in the Jade County valley and saw that it was good.

He walked down Seymour's trail, worn with boot tracks that belonged only to the old man, and stopped at the edge of the river; there the clouds parted to reveal the open face of the mountain, bleached with sunshine and blemishes of snow on rock, which still perished from blight and logger saws, which still had his name written on it in bold, but not unkind, lettering.

As he stooped to touch the water, the mountain lion hopped forth on the opposite bank as if to say, "Time for my morning meeting with John Mark."

It was as giant as John Mark imagined. The tail swished to and fro, thick as a forearm, the yellow eyes lifting in their lantern gleams as he stopped to look with his hand stuck in the water. The boy stood up quick. There, the two of them just stood there like two amiable aliens paying courtesy to each other across a continental divide. He raised the gun and peered through the scope, settling the crosshairs on the cat's face, as if making sure it was real. The mountain lion blinked, licked the water off its whiskers, and swallowed as it cast its gaze farther down the riverbank searching for unfound prey. John Mark cocked the gun and settled his finger on the trigger. He felt the warmth of the Christmas morning on his neck and breathed. His hands trembled. The sunlight and cold beat down on his shoulders and face. His eyes stung and watered. It was Christmas, the mountain a nativity bearing a wild, untamable Christ, and it was good. It was all so good, and so right.

The mountain lion leaped into its home of boulders, and John Mark lowered the gun so the end of the barrel sunk under the surface of the water. Behind him, Keep said, "Going to look for tracks later, if you wanna come."

SEYMOUR

A FOREIGN wind blew in from the North the morning Keep made her decision about the New York college. November brought usual frost that tricks you into thinking winter will be eternal, and the day she made her decision, the woodstove crackled the last of its embers and Justus the cat roosted on a throne of polyester—the cat steals my chair at least once an afternoon, and I don't want to guess the gloomy moods he'll inherit from Keep's absence. To tell the truth, it did not surprise me to hear of her choice. I wanted her to decide and it was a straightforward decision—to stay in the scrape of a dying town she loved or to leave it, to start fresh, to pioneer a new route. I've known for the seventeen years she's been under my roof that she would leave. But I don't suppose the lack of surprise means I went unaffected or wasn't laid bare in the soul. New York is a long way away.

Cities are places of choice. That's why we go to them. The choices pop up everywhere in a place like that. In Jade County, you know what you're getting, no more, no less. Well, I shouldn't quite say that—it sounds cynical. This valley has more to offer the people who take some time for it. For the passerby on his way to Denver, it's a muddy street with stretches of slope either covered in green or blighted pine or mottled and torn by the saws and dozers that rut it daily for Smith and Sophe Lumber Industries. There's a burger joint the high schoolers eat at, the diner, my carpentry and boot shop, Dean Shores' pawn store, a gas station, a post office, and a church, so all I can say without a doubt that the city will rock Keep a bit as a girl who's known nothing else. This valley where she's grown up was named "Jade" for a reason. Sure, it's known for the deep blue hue of the sunrises, and the great spruces that colonnade Church Avenue. But you know they also call it "Jade" because it's so hidden. All you see from a distance is a scarred fold of valley, Keep Mountain's rutted slope, and the town itself obscured by a hedge of pine and fencing. We live in a world hemmed in and nearly ignored by the broader one. Out there she'll be in the hub of the Empire, and God knows she'll grow and bless others, but she'll feel shell shocked at first—that's what wounds my heart to think of. Simply the noise of a city. The constant grinding of gears and footsteps, that ever-resounding thrash of anxiety. Here, she can find the old ways of privacy, and escape the notion that to exist freely and happily you must be staged, seen, applauded. How glad I am she's learned how to exist in the middle of a forest with no eye to notice. If she can live with silence, she can live anywhere.

I noticed her reserve yesterday when we talked about her leaving for college. She said she didn't want to turn back once she decided. It's been weighing on her mind, mostly because she doesn't know how to tell John Mark. Best friends never part easy, of course, and these best friends make up each other's worlds, and have for the past seven years. They met by accident during a snowstorm in the woods. I let Keep go out that day some seven years ago after seeing that look in her eye with her nose pressed up against the window. I told her to meet the cold head on. To have herself an adventure. She has taken this advice to heart far beyond a snowy forest.

She finished the scholarship application in ample time to submit it, and she pestered John Mark to look into Denver schools; I try to encourage the boy to try his best, hope for the best. I always tell him that Jade is beautiful if you've eyes to see and ears to hear.

She went on a walk after finishing the bio report, perhaps over to Church Avenue to meet with John Mark and let him know of her decision. So I thought myself, "Well, this is what it feels like to be an empty nester," and took a walk myself, throwing on my

Carhartt and lighting my pipe on the way. There's a trail that only the mule deer and I share which goes around the town and at one point travels alongside the river for almost two miles. That afternoon, snow had not yet come but was coming, and the ground was brittle with cold. I'm an old man, and even with glasses, don't make out all the dim ins-and-outs of the forest that I otherwise know as well as the back of my hand. Something moved, though, on the other side of the river, once I'd finally got there and stooped down to wash my face in the shallows. A mountain lion dipped its tongue into the water right across from me and took a long drink; it must have been eight feet long, with rippling muscles and a whitish hide almost too pale to be natural. And that tail. It was thick as a forearm and was wrapped around the haunches like a cloak of protection. I've known for some time now that John Mark has been looking nearly night and day for this magnificent creature. Others keep a keen eye out of caution and intrigue. Of course, I can see why. It's not simply the size of the mountain lion but its elusiveness that invites the mystery. You hardly ever see them. And now the mountain lion, once he saw me staring there with a smoldering pipe in hand, leaped over a hedge of sage and bounded into a family of boulders as quickly as it had appeared. The river ran on same as before and already the storm clouds pillaged the sky, promising too much of its treasure.

When I eased through the back door, Keep sat hunched on the couch holding her acceptance letter to the college.

"Hey, snow's on the way," I said.

"So I hear," Keep said. "Where did you go?"

"Ah, just to the river!"

"You're in better shape than I am."

"Very funny." I pointed to the letter. "They're still letting you in, right?"

"Apparently. It's still kind of hard to believe."

"I'm not surprised of it. But I know. It's a lot to take in." She smiled again and set the papers aside. She leaned back against the couch and closed her eyes.

"Where did you run off to? John Mark's?"

I put some water on the stove, wanting coffee.

"No. Just around. I walked by his chop block but he wasn't there yet. I don't know where he is."

"Boy's a mystery."

"Yes," she agreed, rubbing her face with the backs of her hands. "And I don't know how I'm to tell him about this."

"You'll tell him, and it will be hard because it's a hard thing. No sugarcoating it, Keep."

"I know. I know." She took off her coat and went to her bedroom, the cat following her from my armchair.

The emptiness of the house hit me a little.

I went to the toolshed to get my carving knife. I could still see the mountain lion in my mind and felt a glorious impulse to give it some kind of due. A carving. A small carving for John Mark Harrison. Might be a good Christmas gift for the boy.

Inside the shed, it smelled of cut wood and spilt oil, tobacco and coffee, and maybe my old dog, Bishop. The wood floor was knotted and creaked as I walked. A slate of light fell through a big crack in the wall, straight as a knife's edge and making a near perfect division of the space. The light cut that shed in two. It caught all the dust particles that were aroused by my entry, and seemed alive, although so quiet, and so still. I sometimes wonder if moments like these may mean anything—a mountain lion on the other side of a river, a slice of light in a lonesome shed. Sometimes God shows us remarkable ordinaries just so we'll look. Who's to know? I looked then, and smelled cut wood, and remembering my task, went to the back porch and got to work on the carving.

Outside, the back door opened and Keep, humming to herself, walked down the porch steps. Her humming soon melded with the far-off gnashes and thrums of saws and falling timber, as the strips of timber fell off my own knife, making a little woodpile at my feet. I carved and carved the woodblock as they carved and carved the mountain, until Keep came back, safe inside, and I heard the quick cadence of John Mark's footsteps crunching up the hill. He dropped a piece of split wood, stopped to pick it up, and knocked on the door.

ACKNOWLEDGEMENTS

T HIS work would not exist without the help and facilitation of Gina Ochsner and Robert Clark, my writing mentors at Seattle Pacific University. I am also indebted to Scott Cairns, director of the MFA program at SPU, for his encouragement, teachings, and overall spirit of generosity. I'd also like to thank my peers at SPU for their feedback and constructive criticism.

In addition, my parents have always been dedicated readers of my work, and their support has encouraged me to continue writing all these years. Thank you! My two brothers, Josiah and Caleb, along with my sisters-in-law, Cierra and Sallye, have also been nothing but supportive of the process.

There are many others to thank. These include, among others: Cody Weaver, Jacob Lecuyer, Mark Walling, Ryan Kemp, Anthony B. Bradley, Drew Bratcher, Casey Luskin, Sam Hine, Kedrick Nettleton, Joshua Grasso, Jenna Kuhlman & her father Walter, Noah Lawrence, Paul Cardillo, Nichole Beyer, and Avery Stevens. As we learned in the MFA program in Seattle, writing is ultimately a solitary process, but is yet profoundly shaped by community—both present and past. To all those who have helped shape the stories herein, thank you.